Lewis R. Walton

Review and Herald Publishing Association
Washington, D.C.

ISBN 0-8280-0084-0

PRINTED IN U.S.A.

DEDICATION

To Lee R. and Mabel B. Walton, teachers who could make history live.

"To stand in defense of truth and righteousness when the majority forsake us, to fight the battles of the Lord when champions are few—this will be our test."

—Ellen G. White, *Testimonies,* vol. 5, p. 136.

Contents

Foreword

Ω OCCASIONALLY a book is written in such a clear, flowing style that the reader is carried along effortlessly, as on the crest of a wave, from the first chapter to the last. And when the book deals with a subject of current interest, reading it provides maximum pleasure and benefit.

The book in your hands is the kind just described. Before it was published I looked over the manuscript several times, and each time I was impressed by the author's easy style and his ability to hold reader interest.

More than that, I was impressed with his ability to coordinate Adventist history with contemporary national and international events. In quick strokes of his verbal brush he paints a picture that includes happenings in the United States, China, Russia, and Germany as a background for the conflagrations in Battle Creek that destroyed both the sanitarium and the Review and Herald Publishing Association. Thus he places Adventism in a real-life setting, and avoids giving the impression that Adventism exists in a vacuum.

But the writer has done more than demonstrate literary skill; he has come to grips with a subject that should be carefully considered by every Seventh-day Adventist. Ellen White labeled the doctrinal crisis that shook the church at the beginning of the twentieth century as the "alpha" of apostasy and predicted that in due time the "omega" would follow. Perhaps no one knows exactly what she meant by using the term "omega," but Adventists would be irresponsible if they did not seek some understanding of what she had in mind. To be on guard against repeating the mistakes of history, one must learn the lessons that history teaches.

The author of this book suggests various lessons that may be learned from the "alpha" experience, but he is not dogmatic about his conclusions. He draws parallels between the "alpha" and current events within the church, but he does this primarily to stimulate thought, not to end discussion. I think the book provides a helpful perspective on current events by reminding us of "the way the Lord has led us, and His teaching in our past history." It also alerts us to present and future dangers. All who read it thoughtfully and prayerfully will be better prepared to stand loyally for Christ and His truth during the coming crisis.

Kenneth H. Wood, Editor, *Adventist Review*

Prologue

MARK HANNA was a powerful man, bald but handsome, with a thin fringe of hair to frame his face, and when he spoke he was accustomed to seeing results. Just recently, for example, he had almost singlehandedly put William McKinley into the American Presidency. Now a new century had begun. The year 1900 dawned as bright as a new dollar, and so far as Senator Hanna could see, the future was headed straight for the stars. "Furnaces are glowing," he exclaimed. "Spindles are singing their song. Happiness comes to all of us with prosperity!"

The junior Senator from Ohio was not alone in that opinion. On January 1, 1900, the future seemed as full of promise as a spring morning. For once the world was largely at peace. China, with its hundreds of millions, was still open to travel, and to the gospel. Within the huge landmass that her sons and daughters called Great Russia, there was still a little time. To be sure, the hourglass was losing its sand rapidly; great problems would soon cry out for great change. Yet nearly two decades remained before the rattle of gunfire outside the Czar's winter palace would forever turn the course of history—and the opportunities for God's work. Vast changes hung just beyond tomorrow, like the distant gray of a squall line heralding the first approach of an inbound storm, but on New Year's Day, 1900, few people could see anything but the sunlight.

"If one could not have made money this past year, his case is hopeless," exulted one newspaper editor, and a New York clergyman glowed that "laws are becoming more just, rulers humane; music is becoming sweeter and books wiser."

One of the few dissenting voices came from a little 72-year-old lady who happened, this January 1, to be in New South Wales, Australia. For several years Ellen White had been speaking more and more pointedly about some great catastrophe soon to befall the world, and though her remarks seemed generally out of fashion with her times, she held to them with a persistence that demanded notice. "Soon there will be death and destruction, increasing crime, and cruel evil working against the rich who have exalted themselves against the poor. Those who are without God's protection will find no safety in any place or position. Human agents are being trained and are using their inventive power to put in operation the most powerful machinery to wound and to kill. . . . Let the means and the workers be scattered." * Strange words, distinctly out of step with the mood of the day, and much less easy to listen to than the soothing thoughts of the Reverend Newell Hillis, who told his Brooklyn congregation about wiser books and sweeter music. But on the first day of the new century people might have done well to give Ellen White's warnings some careful attention, for she had been right too often in the past to allow one to ignore her and feel really comfortable about it.

No one could possibly have known it that New Year's morning, but Mrs. White's predictions were on the threshold of fulfillment. That very month Lenin would be released from Siberian detention and would race across Russia toward the safety of Western Europe. England, France, and Russia, concerned about the emerging German alliance, were bolstering something called the Triple Entente. And in Zurich, a young college student named Albert Einstein was already writing strange formulas and wondering about the possibility of turning matter into energy.

New Year's Day, 1900—in Shanghai, British steamships turned lazily at their buoys on the Huang-p'u River, basking in the dreamy winter sun. In St. Petersburg, Russia's nobility sped in bright-red sleighs along the banks of the Neva River and then hurried home to dress for the evening. This was the height of what Russian society called the season, a round of glittering nights with white satin gowns and uniforms ablaze with decorations—of parties where "nobody thought of leaving before 3:00 A.M." and the officers stayed until the sky was colored with the pearl, rose, and silver tints of dawn.

New Year's . . . and in Berlin, Count Alfred von Schlieffen already knows that when war comes it will stab across the soft, flat plains of Belgium. He knows, because the maps are already drawn.

And in the writings of the Adventist Church the words reach out in one last, desperate bid for recognition before it is too late: "Human agents are being trained and are using their inventive power to put in operation the most powerful machinery to wound and to kill. . . . Let the means and the workers be scattered."

For the world it seems to be morning, but in the hourglass of history it is nearing sunset, and the sunlight that warms the first day of 1900 is the last golden moment of opportunity to work in peace, fast fading out into night.

God's work can still be done in the sunlight, but time is short. Now only one question really matters: will His people respond?

Chapter 1

"I Would Help You if I Could"

Ω ON JANUARY 1, 1900, Ellen White arose early and—if her usual custom prevailed—took a sponge bath, dressed, and headed promptly for her writing chair. It was a habit borne of many years. The early moments were in many ways the best, free from the distractions of the day's busier hours, and if her early rising was often brought on by painful nights, she had learned how to make the best of the situation. By breakfasttime she usually had several hours of writing behind her.

On this day her mind was burdened with one particular problem, which over the past few years had become a major concern: Where was Dr. John Kellogg taking the Adventist medical work? He was an old friend whose youthful hours had often been spent in the White household, and she liked to write to him "as a mother would write to her son." [1] Yet recently, disturbing things had been happening in Battle Creek, and they seemed to portend trouble. For one thing, against her repeated urging the city had become a large and increasingly unmanageable Adventist colony. For years she had warned against the dangers of concentrating means and talent in one place, yet in 1900 Adventist institutions dominated the city. Near the banks of the Kalamazoo River stood the buildings of the Review and Herald, where management were deeply involved in the practice of job printing for almost any customer willing to pay. A block away the Dime Tabernacle accommodated capacity crowds of 3,400 people. Here 173 Sabbath school classes met each Sabbath morning, factions struggled for control, and for a brief time tithe funds were actually diverted into church operating expense. Within a mile one could find the General Conference offices, Battle Creek College, the growing health-food factory, an orphanage, and a thousand Adventist believers packed into an area so filled with real-estate speculators that amused (and sometimes disgusted) onlookers called it the "Adventist mining camp."[2]

Dwarfing everything was the sprawling Victorian complex called Battle Creek Sanitarium, which stretched for nearly a fifth of a mile along Washington Street and where a thousand employees were, Ellen White warned, beginning to see their calling as little more than a way to make a living. For a church predicated on personal ministry, that was a danger that could hardly be overstated. It meant that in an operational sense, one of the church's major components was dying.

For several years the omens coming out of Battle Creek Sanitarium had been worrisome, studded with hints that the massive institution could actually be lost to denominational control. Kellogg had already shown his colors. Back in 1895, he had established the American Medical Missionary College and had begun to divorce it from the church. "This is not a sectarian school," he had declared, and "sectarian doctrines" would not be taught there.[3]

Now the sanitarium was the strongest force in the church, which implied that if the Adventist Church desired to secure the future of its largest institution, it would have to deal sooner or later with John Harvey Kellogg.

Kellogg was a short, energetic man who in later life scurried around Battle Creek in a white suit and spats and who, it was reported, while riding his bicycle to work, often dictated correspondence to a panting male secretary racing alongside. He was a complex and fascinating character with a natural gift for medicine and an intimidating command of words, a man who could weep while reading Ellen White's letter to a worship group and who could later condemn her as a plagiarist—who could, it seemed, do almost anything except resist the temptation to lead Battle Creek Sanitarium and the entire health message down some mysterious road charted in his own mind. For years Mrs. White had corresponded with the doctor, begging him to call a halt to the ambitious projects in Battle Creek and to send surplus funds out into the world field, particularly to struggling new ventures in Australasia, where lack of money left the work desperately crippled. In reply she had received strange statements that the sanitarium by its charter precluded sending money out of Michigan. It was an ingenious argument, superficially persuasive if one did not understand the potential for legal manipulation in all of this. It was utterly transparent to Ellen White, who may have seen, with a prophet's eye, paneled law offices and shrewd eyes scanning documents, and an intense little man in a white suit calmly sitting while his lawyers did their work, his head tilted back slightly, fingers drumming gently on the arms of his chair. "Matters have been presented before me that have filled my soul with keen anguish," she wrote in 1898. "I saw men linking up arm in arm with lawyers; but God was not in their company. . . . I am commissioned to say to such that you are not moving under the inspiration of the Spirit of God." [4]

The timing of her statement is fascinating. Kellogg had just deftly altered the sanitarium's corporate structure to a form that would allow it, one day, to be voted out of the church. In 1897 its thirty-year charter had expired; under Michigan law the corporation had to be dissolved, its assets sold, and a new association formed. If one wished to introduce change, this had been the unmistakable golden opportunity, and Kellogg had not missed it.

On July 1, 1898, Attorney S. S. Hurlburt and a small crowd of interested people gathered at the courthouse in Marshall, Michigan, where the assets of the sanitarium were sold to a group headed by Kellogg. In turn, they formed a new corporation, adopted bylaws, and issued stock. This had to be done if the sanitarium were to continue, and the General Conference had affirmed the legal steps. Superficially it appeared as if nothing but formalities had been observed, but those who cared to read the new bylaws carefully saw the potential for ominous changes. Stock ownership, once limited to Adventists, was now open to anyone who was willing to sign a document pledging the sanitarium to be "undenominational, unsectarian, humanitarian, and philanthropic." To those who protested such sweeping language Kellogg had a ready answer: it was a mere formality, he said, so that the corporation could enjoy "the advantage of the statutes of the state."[5] (By 1906 the jaws of the trap would be all too evident. Nearing his rupture with the church, the doctor would declare that the corporate charter forbade any activities of sectarian or denominational character, and he would bluntly tell the church what had become of its great dream by the banks of the Kalamazoo River: "The denomination does not own the property, and never can own it, for it belongs *to the public*.")[6]

And now most recently Dr. Kellogg was proposing a new idea, more far-reaching than anything he had yet devised. Put simply, it was the proposition that every church-affiliated sanitarium in America, wherever located, be tied completely to the control of Battle Creek. "In order to bind our different sanitariums together, the Medical Missionary Board has devised this plan," he would soon report, "that instead of creating an entirely independent corporation wherever a sanitarium is organized . . . there shall be auxiliary associations established" that would be "inseparably connected" with Battle Creek.[7]

It was an idea that would be vigorously opposed by Ellen White and church leaders, but in the months ahead voices loyal to Kellogg would praise the concept in a growing chorus of support, for the sanitarium was beginning to attract people dissatisfied with the church. Many of them were gifted men, trained in theology or medicine. Some had traveled and preached with Ellen White. At least one was a songwriter whose hymns had once captured the spirit of the Advent message. Some of these dissidents—financed, it was rumored, from the rich cash flow in the sanitarium—would begin putting together a book denouncing Mrs. White as a fraud. Prominent figures would speak with growing boldness of a great transformation in the church, of some new form of structure, of new objectives and a whole new mission. And meanwhile, little by little beneath the surface, protected by Battle Creek's wealth and by John Kellogg's capacity for persuasion, the dissenters would press ahead toward goals still carefully hidden from all except the eyes of a 72-year-old woman in Australia who saw, as she slept, strange meetings and nighttime conferences, and a white-suited man with a power of persuasion unexplainable in human terms.

And that is the problem that burdens Ellen White's mind as the new year's sunrise warms the summer sky over Cooranbong. The great medical arm of the church, so necessary to break down prejudice and to open doors to the Advent message, is being separated inexorably from the main body of Adventist thought. Mrs. White takes a clean piece of paper, lifts her pen, and the words begin to flow to President George Irwin of the General Conference: "Dear Brother Irwin: . . . Save Dr. Kellogg from himself. He is not heeding the counsel he should heed."[8]

Nineteen hundred—and the opportunities to finish God's work have never been brighter. For once the world is almost entirely at peace. From Maine to Manila, from Paris to Canton, one can go almost anywhere with the gospel, and without even a passport. Hungry for a health message most of them have never heard, people seek outdoor exercise and turn their unmet needs into a mad craze for bicycling. The fortunate few who can get to Battle Creek come by the thousands, unaware of the struggles that roil beneath the surface, thrilled even with a partial view of truth. Toiling angels have done all that heaven can do to prepare the world for the Advent message. The great latter-rain message of victory in Jesus has been offered. In America national Sunday legislation has been introduced, widely debated, raised like a beacon to galvanize idling believers into new life. It is inconceivable that such an opportunity can be missed, and yet it is happening. The Battle Creek Sanitarium is on a departure course from the church, its funds misapplied, its legal structure manipulated. At the Review and Herald, worldly material is being accepted for printing. The contents are such that Mrs. White fears that even the men who read it casually while setting type will be endangered. The basic theology of the church is beginning to be challenged by unorthodox ideas about the nature of God—ideas that, she warns, will threaten such basic truths as the heavenly sanctuary. Desperate to protect the church from danger, hardly knowing how, she warns Adventist parents to keep their children away from Battle Creek, where they may be "leavened by the insinuations . . . introduced to weaken confidence in our ministers and message." [9] The last moments of sunlight are slipping away from God's people as they buy and sell real estate property, and build additions to the Battle Creek Sanitarium, and plan, and plan . . .

Soon a letter, penned by Ellen White a few days before Christmas, will reach Dr. Kellogg's desk. "I write to you as a mother would write to her son. I would help you if I could. . . . I would go to see you if I could. . . . If you receive the messages of warning sent you, you will be saved from great trial." [10]

Everything is so ready. Like Israel at Sinai, God's people are now only a few weeks' travel from the Promised Land.

It is time for the Advent message to go like fire in a hayfield.

It is time for the devil's counterattack.

It is time for an apostasy called the alpha.

Chapter 2

"We Received the Sad News"

ON FEBRUARY 18, 1902—in the cold predawn hours the alarm gong sounded inside the brick-and-stone arches of the Battle Creek Fire Department. Lights flickered on; men fumbled with the brass buttons on their clumsy, double-breasted coats while downstairs harnesses dropped onto the engine horses. A driver swung himself onto the seat of the pump engine, grabbed a handful of reins, and the big machine clattered out over the brick pavement, shattering the silence of a black winter morning. It was Tuesday, and the Battle Creek Sanitarium was burning to the ground.

On the grounds the night staff successfully led the four hundred patients to safety while the main building became a pillar of flames. A fireman would later remark how futile his efforts seemed to be; water poured on the flames seemed only to add to their fury. By dawn most of the great complex was gone, reduced to steaming ruins beneath the winter sky.

Dr. Kellogg, returning from the Pacific Coast, learned about the tragedy from a news reporter at the Chicago railroad depot. He went into immediate action. After boarding the Battle Creek train, Kellogg had his secretary procure a table, and he spent the rest of the trip sketching plans for a new building.

"To-day we received the sad news of the burning of the Battle Creek Sanitarium," Ellen White wrote two days later, but she expressed no surprise. For many weeks she had worried about events in Battle Creek, her nights made "very restless" by a premonition of coming trouble, and now she was at a loss for words. "I would at this time speak words of wisdom, but what can I say? We are afflicted with those whose life interests are bound up in this institution. . . . We can indeed weep with those who weep."[1] She did, however, have some advice to offer that put her on a direct collision course with Dr. Kellogg: under no circumstances rebuild at Battle Creek. Instead, construct a number of smaller institutions. "A solemn responsibility rests upon those who have had charge of the Battle Creek Sanitarium. Will they build up in Battle Creek a mammoth institution, or will they carry out the purpose of God by making plants in many places?"[2]

It was a question that would be answered very soon. On March 17, 1902, a large group of church leaders met at Battle Creek to plan what to do next. Kellogg was there, bright with enthusiasm, painting verbal pictures of a magnificent new building, and though Ellen White's warnings were less than a month old, a plan was devised that some of the brethren may have seen as a sort of compromise. Instead of replacing both major buildings, only one would be erected, limited to five stories in height and 450 feet in length. Only later, on inspecting the foundation footings, would they discover how loosely Kellogg intended to interpret his restrictions.

That discovery, however, remained for the future, and meanwhile a plan had to be devised to raise the money for construction. A. G. Daniells, president of the General Conference, recalled that Ellen White had recently dedicated her book *Christ's Object Lessons* for the purpose of raising money for Adventist schools. It had been quite successful, and Daniells wondered whether Kellogg, a nationally famous health lecturer, might write a popular medical book to raise the funds needed to rebuild the sanitarium. Kellogg under-took the job with gusto. He was a prolific writer, who dictated on the train, from his bicycle, even from the bathtub to a male secretary who seems to have functioned reasonably well despite the distracting circumstances. Enthusiastically he undertook the task and completed the manuscript for the new book in record time; then he left for an extended summer vacation in Europe.

So the die was cast. Battle Creek Sanitarium would be rebuilt notwithstanding Ellen White's advice, and the brethren would soon learn that they were playing a game in which the stakes were high and the rules mysterious. Inspecting the founda-tions one day in early summer, someone discovered a curious fact: they were 100 feet longer than Kellogg had promised, and now it appeared that several large wings would extend in a semicircle from the rear of the building. In 1904 Ellen White's words summarized the situation with poignant sadness: "When the Lord swept the large Sanitar-ium out of the way at Battle Creek, He did not design that it should ever be built there again. . . . Had this counsel been heeded, the heavy responsibilities connected with the Battle Creek Sanitarium would not now exist. These responsibilities are a terrible burden."[3]

The "terrible burden" to which she referred was, of course, financial. Kellogg was rebuilding on a grand scale, far in excess of anything the brethren had imagined, and it was beginning to be expensive. The building on Washington Street was materializ-ing into a massive Italian renaissance structure capable of accommodating more than one thousand patients—some ten times the number Mrs. White suggested as ideal. There were five acres of glis-tening floor space, with marble inlays installed by the same skilled Italian artisan who had supervised the gorgeous mosaic work at the Library of Con-gress, and it appeared that nothing would be spared to make the place "the most complete, thoroughly equipped, and perfect establishment of the sort in the world."[4] The financial load imposed by such plans soon grew staggering.

But the real crisis for the church, so terrible that Ellen White would openly wonder whether she could live through it, involved something deeper than money. Few could see it, but it had already arrived. Hidden in Dr. Kellogg's new book were all the elements of an unparalleled crisis in doctrine.

For several years Kellogg had been making some rather odd statements about the nature of God. "God is in me," he had told a General Conference meeting recently, "and everything I do is God's power; every single act is a creative act of God."[5] It was a fascinating idea that seemed to bring the Deity very near, and it quickly captured the interest of some well-known denominational thinkers. There was a peculiar charm about Kellogg's suggestion that the air we breathe is the medium through which God sends His Holy Spirit physically into our lives, that the sunlight is His visible "Shekinah." And even well-trained minds responded to the new concept, catching fire from Kellogg's evangelical enthusiasm. Now these sentiments were appearing even more persuasively in the galley sheets of the new book he had chosen to call The Living Temple. In the human body, he asserted, was "the Power which builds, which creates—it is God Himself, the divine Presence in the temple."[6]

Few people realized that this idea could take one clear out of Christianity, into a realm of religious mysticism that had no room for the Divine Being or a place called heaven. One man who saw the danger was William Spicer, a recently returned missionary from India, now a General Conference officer, who instantly recognized in Kellogg's new theology the same ideas he had seen in Hinduism. Alarmed, Spicer went to Kellogg to straighten it all out with a personal chat. The two men sat down on the veranda of the rambling twenty-seven-room house that Kellogg called The Residence, and Spicer, to his surprise, found himself "at once in the midst of a discussion of the most controversial questions."

"Where is God?" Kellogg asked.

"He is in heaven," Spicer replied. "There the Bible pictures the throne of God, and all the heavenly beings at His command."

Kellogg, 50 years of age and 13 years Spicer's senior, swept his arm in a gesture toward the lawn, declaring that God was in the grass, the trees, the plants, everything about them.

"Where is heaven?" he asked.

"In the center of the universe," Spicer replied. "Where that is, one cannot say."

"Heaven is where God is, and God is everywhere," Kellogg retorted. Spicer left the interview stunned, realizing that he had glimpsed the tip of something larger than anyone had imagined—something that could shake the church. "There was no place in this scheme of things for angels going between heaven and earth. . . . The cleansing of the sanctuary . . . was not something in a far-away heaven." The heart was "the Sanctuary to be cleansed."[7]

William Spicer had encountered the first winds of the storm, and he read their awful meaning accurately. In the summer of 1902, while the world stood ready for the third angel's message and the last moments of peaceful opportunity dribbled away, one of the main pillars of the Adventist faith had suddenly been challenged. In a way that he did not fully understand himself, Kellogg had assailed the very rationale for Adventism. He had, perhaps unknowingly at first, attacked the doctrine of the heavenly sanctuary.

At the very heart of Seventh-day Adventist doctrine stood the concept that in the year 1844 a great event had taken place in heaven. Adventists based that belief on their understanding of the prophecies in Daniel 8 and 9, in which 2300 years of prophetic time began with the decree of a Persian king and ended in the fall of 1844. In the troubled autumn of that year they had reviewed those prophecies, seeking to understand why Christ had not come as the Millerite preachers had predicted. Their research led them to a new understanding of the book of Daniel and to a theology never before understood in the Christian world. Deep study and fervent prayer had brought them to the conclusion that in October of 1844 Christ had entered the Most Holy Compartment of the great heavenly sanctuary, of which the ancient Jewish tabernacle had once been a model. There He had commenced the climactic phase of redeeming the human race. In the holiest of all possible settings He had begun reviewing the lives of all individuals who had ever claimed salvation in His name.

It was a solemn idea, even when one thought only about judgment of those already dead, but Adventists came to see a more challenging thought: at some point, potentially soon enough to confront the generation living in 1844, Christ's judgment review would pass from the dead to those still living. When that work was completed, there would be a final act of catastrophic importance to the human race. Christ would drop the censer symbolizing His ministry of mercy on behalf of man, and would utter the words found in Revelation 22:11: "He that is unjust, let him be unjust still . . . he that is holy, let him be holy still." Human probation, usually thought of as ending at death, would, for a generation of human beings, close while they were yet alive. Everything in Adventism pointed toward that event, warned of it, begged people to prepare for it. The Advent message of 1844 was an electrifying call, calculated to shatter earthly security and to get people ready to meet the Lord. And unless one were willing to commit everything, sacrificing all that human instinct deemed important, it was a concept that could leave one enormously uncomfortable.

Almost from the moment of its birth, the Adventist sanctuary doctrine had come under attack. Theologians ridiculed it as a transparent attempt to explain away the fact that Christ had not returned in 1844. Others, perhaps unintentionally, had attacked in more subtle ways. It was terribly challenging to realize that one's life might soon be under God's final review. From every quarter the attacks had come, so persistent and intense that Ellen White finally said that "for the past fifty years every phase of heresy has been brought to bear upon us, to becloud our minds regarding the teaching of the word—especially concerning the ministration of Christ in the heavenly sanctuary, and the message of heaven for these last days, as given by the angels of the fourteenth chapter of Revelation."[8] And she had cried out, "God forbid that the clatter of words coming from human lips should lessen the belief of our people in the truth that there is a sanctuary in heaven, and that a pattern of this sanctuary was once built on this earth."[9]

Some of the loudest "clatter," as Ellen White chose to call it, had come from a prominent Adventist minister by the name of D. M. Canright, who had flirted for years with questions and doubts and had assumed anti-Adventist doctrine. He finally left the church altogether, thereafter making it his mission in life to attack his former beliefs. In 1889 he had published a book entitled *Seventh-day Adventism Renounced,* in which he had charged that "Seventh-day Adventists make everything turn upon their view of the sanctuary. . . . If they are wrong on this, their whole theory breaks down."[10] Having said that, he next proceeded to an attack on Ellen White, followed by assaults on the Sabbath, the law, and the state of the dead. Nearing the end of his 418 pages, Canright reached his conclusion: "The system of Seventh-day Adventism rests for its foundation on the unsupported theories of an uneducated old farmer in his last days and the reveries of a totally uneducated, unread, sickly, excitable girl."[11] But Canright's brief day in the sun had ended, and he found himself with nothing except lonely memories of what might have been. In

1919, with the shadows of his last illness deepening about him, he would reach out from the twilight into which he was descending for one last appeal to his brother. "Stay with the message, Jasper. I left and I know I am dying, a lost man."[12]

Canright had chosen to attack the sanctuary truth frontally, charging that Adventists had misinterpreted Daniel 8:14 and had mistakenly linked it with Leviticus 16, which describes the Jewish Day of Atonement. Christ had gone directly into the Most Holy Place at His ascension, Canright argued, and hence Adventist emphasis on the cleansing of the sanctuary in 1844 was wrong. It was, to repeat, a direct attack on the church's basic beliefs; it took no special gift to read his book and see that he disagreed with Adventism.

But the newest challenge*to the sanctuary, coming from John Harvey Kellogg in 1902, was anything but obvious. It led one through a series of seemingly logical steps, each somewhat concealed from the next, so that it was possible to find oneself deeply afield from Adventism before realizing that anything was wrong. For many people who longed to know God better, it was reassuring to see Him in the sunlight, feel Him in the air one breathed, and believe that He was in every act of life. Yet if a person cared to think about it, all this produced some questions that were difficult to answer within the framework of traditional Adventism—questions that William Spicer had already encountered on Kellogg's veranda. If God is everywhere, and if heaven is where God is, then heaven must also be everywhere. If that is so, where *is* the sanctuary? Kellogg had an answer, of course: it was found in the title of his new book *The Living Temple*. God's sanctuary was in the human body—a step in logic that now compelled one to discard the events of 1844 as an irrelevance unsuited to new light. At best, 1844 could be explained only as a fact of history, a way station on Adventism's road toward maturity.

It was a subtle error not even completely under-

stood by the doctor himself, and yet some denominational leaders were recognizing it; and the
question that was now beginning to spread around
Battle Creek was this: Should Kellogg's new book
even be printed? It was not a simple problem. As
1902 waned, the expensive sanitarium construction
was threatening a full-blown financial crisis. For
monetary reasons, Dr. Kellogg's book badly needed
to be published and sold. Then, too, there were a
good many people around Battle Creek who saw
nothing wrong with the book at all, and who were
adopting the doctor's theology with evangelical
gusto. It was a stormy atmosphere in which the
General Conference Committee met in the fall of
1902 to decide whether to issue a printing order to
the manager of the Review and Herald.

Their decision was not rendered easy by the
report of the review committee who had been
appointed to read the manuscript and recommend
whether it be printed or scrubbed; the majority of
that group saw "no reason why it may not be
recommended," [13] a report signed by men such as A.
T. Jones, who had traveled and preached with Ellen
White in the years after 1888. Only two of the five
committee members voted against the book.

And then occurred one of those unusual events
that forever turns the course of history, altering the
relationships between men and institutions. The
Autumn Council of 1902 accepted the minority
report; the book would not be published, and the
church would simply trust the Lord that funds for
the new sanitarium could be found.

By all denominational norms and practices, that
should have been the end of the story. But in 1902 Dr.
John Kellogg was nearing a point of no return. For
several years he had rejected messages from Ellen
White that crossed his plans, usually with the
excuse that she had acted on false information
supplied by his foes and that her testimonies to him
were mistaken. Now he was faced with a direct
challenge from the organized church, and he had to

make a decision. Quickly he seized an alternative: Didn't the Review accept outside printing orders? A message went down Washington Street to the Adventist Central Publishing House: print 5,000 copies of *The Living Temple* and charge the job to J. H. Kellogg.

The order was accepted. The type being held for approval of the book was ready for use. Plates were ready for the press. In the pressroom neat piles of paper stood ready for the bite of the big steam press. In a quiet California valley Ellen White went to bed troubled by a premonition she understood all too well. "In the visions of the night I have seen an angel standing with a sword as of fire stretched over Battle Creek." [14]

For the Review, time could now be measured in hours.

Chapter 3

"A Sword as of Fire"

ARTHUR G. DANIELLS, the 44-year-old leader of the General Conference, worked late on the evening of December 30, 1902. During a few moments' break, he chatted first with his young administrative assistant and then with I. H. Evans, general manager of the Review and Herald Publishing Company. It was a warm evening as Michigan winters went, snowless and quiet, and the two men may well have been relaxed and congenial in their conversation. The Review, largest and most modern publishing house in Michigan, was doing exceptionally well. The old year had produced a handsome profit and the new year promised to be just as bright.

From two blocks up Washington Street the tabernacle bell announced prayer meeting, and Daniells may have glanced at his watch to discover that it was now seven-thirty. If so, it was the last normal act Daniells would perform that night. Moments later the lights went out; from across the street came a lurid glow that was unmistakable to anyone who had seen the sanitarium fire. The Review and Herald main building was aflame.

By the time Daniells and Evans reached the street, the entire pressroom was ablaze. It was a furious sight, broken by periodic explosions as the windows blew out of superheated offices. From outside one could hear the sound of machinery falling as the second floor collapsed. Within an hour the Review and Herald Publishing Company was gone, a pile of charcoal and scattered brick, with broken Adventist presses lying among the melted plates of Kellogg's *Living Temple*.

Gone. Within one devastating year the two major institutions of the Seventh-day Adventist Church had disappeared in smoke, and Chief Weeks, of the Battle Creek Fire Department, summed it all up as well as anyone could: "There is something strange about your SDA fires, with the water poured on acting more like gasoline."[1] For weeks an eerie reminder hung over Battle Creek, making it impossible to forget what had happened. During the blaze a large coal pile had caught fire. It burned clear into February, producing a column of smoke that reminded, mutely, of Ellen White's warning: "Unless there is a reformation, calamity will overtake the publishing house, and the world will know the reason."[2] And now it had happened, and the message was painted in the Michigan sky for weeks.

"For many years I have carried a heavy burden for our institutions," Mrs. White wrote after receiving the sad telegram. "Sometimes I have thought I would attend no more large gatherings for our people, for my messages seem to leave little impression on the minds of our leading brethren after the meetings have closed." She told rather mournfully how she left such meetings "pressed down as a cart beneath sheaves."[3] The smoky message over Battle Creek came down to one very simple issue: Would God's people, even at the expense of their own plans and preferences, follow the instructions given by His messenger?

That was a question that John Harvey Kellogg seemed very close to answering irrevocably. He had been warned repeatedly by Ellen White that his new theological ideas would lead him and all who followed him onto perilous ground. The organized church had refused to print his manuscript. He had proceeded on his own, and now the wreckage of the Review and Herald Publishing Company lay be-

neath a column of coal smoke that smudged the
wintry sky. By any measure of judgment there was a
message here for Dr. Kellogg; yet he was about to
demonstrate the power of a choice that, having
rejected truth, now led ever further from it. One of
his first acts after the fire was to take his manuscript
to an outside publisher for printing.

Kellogg had embarked on a direct challenge to
church leadership, and it soon became clear that
the game might involve more than just the printing
of one book—might, in fact, involve control of the
General Conference itself.

The Seventh-day Adventist Church was organized as a democratic system. Local churches elected
officers by majority vote. Periodically they also
elected members to conference constituency meetings, where delegates represented their church in
electing conference officers and a conference exec-
utive committee. Local conferences, in turn, sent
representatives to constituency meetings, where
union officers were elected. And, periodically, the
General Conference went into formal session,
where the same democratic process was employed
to elect world leadership.

It was a workable system, similar to democratic
governments throughout the world, but it shared
with them a common reality: it was not immune from
manipulation by those who were politically skilled
and highly organized. Thus a well-structured local
group could send to the conference constituency
meeting delegates who might not really represent
the thinking of the church as a whole, but who could
speak for a particular viewpoint or theology so
skillfully that the direction of even a large conference could be significantly affected. And there is
every indication that in 1903 John Harvey Kellogg
was going through this precise pattern of reasoning.
Bewildering conflicts began to develop in Battle
Creek. Political factions centering upon the sanitarium in time even struggled for control of the Battle
Creek tabernacle; rumors ran deep; old friendships

suffered. The Dime Tabernacle began to develop the classic symptoms of a church in trouble.

Meanwhile, there were signs that Kellogg was also trying to unseat the leadership of the General Conference. From 1901 to 1903 there was no formal General Conference presidency; instead there was a committee of twenty-five men who chose a "chairman." Under ideal circumstances this type of organization might have worked well enough, but it contained a weakness readily visible to anyone with political skill and a bit of ambition: the leader of the world church was no longer selected and given a mandate by the General Conference acting in session; he was appointed by twenty-four other men. Control thirteen of them, and you could put anyone you wished into office.

Kellogg was not known for missing such opportunities, and 1902 and 1903 proved to be no exception. He began an intense campaign to have A. G. Daniells removed from General Conference leadership, and though his plan ultimately failed, the doctor did recruit a coalition of powerful, articulate men who fully supported his theology and thought that his views ought to be promulgated in the church in the widest possible way. They were "men of prominence," as Daniells would later describe them—ministers, physicians, and educators who "openly took their position in favor of the book and of its teachings."[4] And toward summer both Daniells and Ellen White were jolted when they realized that this group of strong, persuasive minds was making a point of going after the one resource that the church could not afford to lose—its youth.

For those committed to major changes in the status quo, young people have always been a tempting target of opportunity. If change cannot be accomplished at the first try, there is always the hope of reaching the youth, whose fascination for new and unconventional ideas might be used to advantage in producing a more sympathetic "next generation." (That tactic was just becoming evident in Eastern Europe, where forces committed to political change had tried and failed to change the system and so had begun an aggressive appeal to youth; time would show how effective their technique would be.) Ellen White was acutely aware of the power that young people could contribute to the church; she talked wistfully about a great youth "army" that would carry the gospel to the "whole world,"[5] and she instantly recognized trouble when it became clear that Kellogg's forces were beginning to look with interest at the church's young people.

The first hint of that tactic was revealed when Kellogg's book came off the press. *The Living Temple* was immediately promoted and sent to local conferences just in time for the summer camp meeting season, and "energetic efforts" were made to involve the youth in circulating it for sale.[6] Elder Daniells noted the new development with great concern. "I saw seeds being sown among the hundreds of young people in our leading institutions," he reported, something that he "firmly believed would produce results heartbreaking to hundreds of our brethren."[7]

Kellogg was also using young people in a political way. In November of 1903 Ellen White wrote to Elder S. N. Haskell, warning him that students were being enlisted in a letter-writing campaign to produce political pressure favorable to the sanitarium. "At the sanitarium in Battle Creek, the students and helpers have been encouraged by the managers to write to their parents and friends and tell of wonderful things being done in the institution," she said—things that had been revealed to her as being far from wonderful.[8] She constantly worried about the young students at the sanitarium, who were hearing the new theology from professors whom they respected, and the dangers were so great that she openly warned parents to keep their children away from Battle Creek. Back in 1901, in response to her concern, the college had been closed and the school moved to new quarters at Berrien Springs, leaving in Battle Creek only the medically related classes taught in the sanitarium. The Charter for Battle Creek College had not expired, however, leaving the theoretical possibility of reopening the campus anytime someone wanted to do so, and now as the battle heated up, Kellogg seized on this technicality as a way to reach the young people of the church. Attractive brochures were printed up announcing the reopening of Battle Creek College (a necessity, he maintained, for accreditation technicalities related to the medical school). Teams of recruiters took to the field. Grandiose plans for the new institution were laid, and the youth were told about the "great advantages of training in this reopened Battle Creek College."[9] It was a challenge that brought Mrs. White to her feet in alarm.

"How could we consent to have the flower of our youth called to Battle Creek to receive their education, when God has given warning after warning that they are not to go there," she cried out. Some of the instructors "do not understand the real groundwork of our faith. . . . God forbid that one word of encouragement should be spoken to call our youth to a place where they will be leavened by misrepresentations and falsehoods regarding the testimonies, and the work and character of the ministers of God."[10] Thus the issues, according to Mrs. White, were two: belief in the Spirit of Prophecy and support for the ministry of the organized church. And to send young people to Battle Creek would expose them to attacks on both.

There was a growing possibility that it would expose them to another danger as well. Early in the history of Adventism, departures from basic doctrine had been accompanied by bizarre behavior patterns, and now similar problems seemed to be arising. "There were confusing ideas of free love," Elder L. H. Christian would later recall, "and there were immoral practices by some of those who presented the doctrine of an impersonal God diffused through nature, and the doctrine of holy flesh. The details of that chapter of shame should not now be told, but those who knew the facts understood the truth of these words:

"'Pantheistic theories are not sustained by the Word of God. . . . Darkness is their element, sensuality their sphere. They gratify the natural heart, and give leeway to inclination.'—*Review and Herald,* Jan. 21, 1904, p. 9." [11]

Those who accepted Kellogg's ideas seemed to adopt a mood of aggressive evangelism that could rapidly turn to belligerence if thwarted. One evening Elder Daniells was walking home from an Autumn Council meeting of the General Conference Committee. It was October of 1903; the matter of Kellogg's book (now printed, against denominational advice) had become an intense, emotional controversy in the church. Beneath a glowing streetlamp, Daniells stopped to talk for a few minutes with a worker who believed Kellogg's views and who was doing "all in his power" to circulate the book. The two men chatted awhile, no doubt trying to convert each other, when suddenly the worker's disposition turned sour. "You are making the mistake of your life," he threatened. "After all this turmoil, some of these days you will wake up to find yourself rolled in the dust, and another will be leading the forces."

"I do not believe your prophecy," Daniells replied, and then he blurted an afterthought, in the language of a man who seems to have just glimpsed something larger than his own career. "At any rate, I would rather be rolled in the dust doing what I believe in my soul to be right than to walk with princes, doing what my conscience tells me is wrong." And then he turned toward his front door to salvage what rest he could from the troubled night, no doubt musing on the strange behavioral changes that accompanied his friends' forays into this new theology. [12]

That, if one stopped to think about it, was one of the greatest dangers that now faced the church. In the last analysis, the message of Adventism had always included behavior. Fear God, and give glory to Him. Remember the Sabbath day, to keep it holy. Blessed are they that do His commandments. To him that overcometh. *To him that overcometh . . .*

There was nothing comfortable in the Advent message for anyone who cared to accept Christianity halfway. "Those who are living upon the earth when the intercession of Christ shall cease in the sanctuary above are to stand in the sight of a holy God without a mediator. Their robes must be spotless, their characters must be purified from sin by the blood of sprinkling. Through the grace of God and their own diligent effort they must be conquerors in the battle with evil. While the investigative judgment is going forward in heaven, while the sins of penitent believers are being removed from the sanctuary, there is to be a special work of purification, of putting away of sin, among God's people upon earth."[13]

Adventism had taken people further than they had ever gone before, into the very heart of heaven, to a room where dazzling light hovered over a place called the mercy seat, and where one also rediscovered an eternal constant called the law of God. Here the final act in the plan of salvation was now in progress; from this place came not only mercy but a new challenge to human behavior, and a power, born of faith, to live the victorious life. *"Through the grace of God and their own diligent effort they must be conquerors in the battle with evil."*[14]

This was Adventism's unique contribution to the world, a final message that put the capstone on the Reformation. For centuries Christians had believed that salvation comes from faith in Christ. Fully accepting this, Adventists drew from the Scriptures a new dimension that plumbed the very depths of faith: through faith in Christ the entire life could be brought into harmony with the divine law that held the universe together.

And all of this was said with a sense of urgency, as though one's time in which to accomplish it might be very short. "We are preparing to meet Him who, escorted by a retinue of holy angels, is to appear in the clouds of heaven to give the faithful and the just the finishing touch of immortality. When He comes He is not to cleanse us of our sins, to remove from us the defects in our characters, or to cure us of the infirmities of our tempers and dispositions. If wrought for us at all, this work will all be accomplished before that time. When the Lord comes, those who are holy will be holy still."[15] On a summer day in 1868 Ellen White had written similar thoughts in a birthday letter to her son, in which a mother's love had blended with the unmistakable challenge of the old Advent message: "Be not deceived. God is not mocked. Nothing but holiness will prepare you for heaven. . . . The heavenly character must be acquired on earth, or it can never be acquired at all."[16]

There was an idealism about Adventism, something beyond even the dreams of the Reformers, who had lightened the world with the reawakened message of faith. Luther, Calvin, Knox—all had lived in the ragged ending of history's long night, each pushing back the shadows in his own way, as God gave him strength. But now the day, begun so full of promise in the sixteenth century, was far spent. Human history was nearly ended, and Seventh-day Adventists had a message that had never before been given to the world. This generation might live through the investigative judgment—might live to see Jesus come.

Thus Adventist attention tended to focus on goals that could no longer be put into some comfortably distant future. For them the challenge was now, and they looked into the Bible for examples of what God expected from people who might be translated to heaven without passing through the grave. "By the translation of Enoch the

Lord designed to teach an important lesson," Ellen White wrote. "Men were taught that it is possible to obey the law of God; that even while living in the midst of the sinful and corrupt, they were able, by the grace of God, to resist temptation, and become pure and holy. . . . The godly character of this prophet represents the state of holiness which *must be attained* by those who shall be 'redeemed from the earth' (Revelation 14:3) at the time of Christ's second advent."[17] And that standard seemed to be a part of the very mission of the church.

Enoch had lived upon the earth before its destruction by water, his life itself a message of mercy, showing God's power to save. Now an even greater destruction awaited, and the world deserved one last clear view of the character of God. "Like Enoch, they will warn the world of the Lord's second coming and of the judgments to be visited upon transgression, and by their holy conversation and example they will condemn the sins of the ungodly."[18] In 1902 she had again reminded Adventists that "not all the books written can serve the purpose of a holy life. Men will believe, not what the minister preaches, but what the church lives."[19]

Adventists, after all, had made one of the most daring assertions ever made in the Christian faith. They claimed to have a new view into the deepest recesses of heaven, where one found the standard by which Jesus was even now judging the world. Adventists had rediscovered the law, and now they had to do something with it: they either had to live it, through the power of God, or develop the world's best excuses for sinning.

There was a real danger that they might be tempted to choose the latter alternative. The standard that revealed itself in the sanctuary was, after all, exceedingly high. And Ellen White warned against this possibility in terms that are difficult to misunderstand. "Let no one say, I cannot remedy my defects of character. If you come to this decision, you will certainly fail of obtaining everlasting life."[20] In the important year of 1888, she had written similar thoughts. "Through defects in the character, Satan works to gain control of the whole mind, and he knows that if these defects are cherished, he will succeed. Therefore he is constantly seeking to deceive the followers of Christ with his fatal sophistry that it is impossible for them to overcome."[21] It was a startling warning, directed at the dangers that would result if Adventists ever decided to make excuses for the law rather than to keep it; and yet, as always, her message ended on a note of hope: "Let none, then, regard their defects as incurable. God will give faith and grace to overcome them."[22] And the comforting assurance is given: "When it is in the heart to obey God, when efforts are put forth to this end, Jesus accepts this disposition and effort as man's best service, and He makes up for the deficiency with His own divine merit. But He will not accept those who claim to have faith in Him, and yet are disloyal to His Father's commandment."[23] *1SM382*

 COL 331

 GC 489

Thus there seemed to be a special mission for people who called themselves Seventh-day Adventists, who knew so much about what would soon happen to the world. For centuries Christians had trumpeted the message of faith; now Adventists were pushing that message to its furthest limits, demanding from faith the ultimate that it could bring: an Elijah message, a message that began on earth and ended in heaven. Anything that challenged that message of personal victory and personal witness also questioned the very mission of the church.

And therein lay the danger in Kellogg's teachings of 1903. "Those doctrines, followed to their logical conclusion, sweep away the whole Christian economy," Mrs. White warned. "They teach that the scenes just before us are not of sufficient importance to be given special attention."[24] The church and the world were plunging through deepening evening toward something called the close of probation, prior to which every individual would be examined by God "with as close and searching scrutiny as if there were not another being upon the earth."[25] When that event arrived, the destiny of all would be eternally decided for life or death. It was a challenge that was impossible to overstate.

Yet Adventists were being lulled by pleasing theories about the nature of God, in which the awesome sanctuary truths faded from sight and the Shekinah became nothing more than springtime's sunlight. Desperate to warn the church, alarmed by the fascinating power of error, Ellen White searched for some way to illustrate how easily one could mistake error for truth, and she resorted to the optical illusion of two railroad tracks, blending in the distance until they seemed to be one. "The track of truth lies close beside the track of error, and both tracks may seem to be one to minds which are not worked by the Holy Spirit."[26]

And then, seeing some of the church's best minds caught in the trap, leading others into it with powers of eloquence that had once been devoted to the Advent message, she cried out in nearly total despair: "My soul is so greatly distressed as I see the working out of the plans of the tempter that I cannot express the agony of my mind. Is the church of God always to be confused by the devices of the accuser, when Christ's warnings are so definite, so plain?"[27]

Together with the church she loved, Ellen White was now descending into a crisis so great that she wondered whether she could live through it. The year 1904 faded toward 1905. Four precious years had passed, years of peace and plenty, and the church that should have trumpeted its message to the world instead struggled against attacks on the most basic truths. Its greatest institution teetered on the brink of loss. (It *would* be lost just a few months hence, in 1906.) The Spirit of Prophecy was under a crescendo of attack, both openly and secretly, by able minds who were funded, it was rumored, from the cash flow of the Battle Creek

Sanitarium. Even the Battle Creek tabernacle, built with dimes contributed by faithful members and the interested citizenry of Battle Creek, was the subject of a struggle for control. And, meanwhile, errors were being offered as new light, in a form so subtle that they confused both college students and seasoned workers. Like a ship, the church was now moving through a foggy, treacherous ocean that Ellen White saw filled with icebergs.

At Port Arthur, Admiral Heihachiro orders the Japanese fleet into battle formation, unleashes his thunder, and blows the Russian Baltic fleet out of existence. Russia surrenders southern Manchuria; Japan, her power unchallenged, occupies Korea. The balance of power in Asia tumbles, and things will never again be the same. Events are now in motion that will not cease until nearly half the world is closed, for a time, to the gospel.

For the church, the challenges are just beginning.

It is time for the second prong of Satan's attack.

It is time for Albion Fox Ballenger.

Chapter 4

"You Are the Man . . . "

ON MARCH 16, 1905, President Daniells, of the General Conference, wrote to Elder William White, who was then in California, regarding a disturbing problem. A minister, recently sent to England as an evangelist and mission superintendent, had begun saying some odd things about the sanctuary doctrine—ideas similar to those that had taken D. M. Canright out of the church eighteen years before. Apparently the evangelist was developing quite a following; churches in Ireland, Wales, northern England—just about anywhere the man had been—were now in turmoil. In Birmingham and other places, ministers were having " 'serious difficulty' " with " 'some of the leading brethren on the subject of the sanctuary.' "[1] Elder Eugene W. Farnsworth, trying desperately to patch up the damage, was nearly beside himself, and he had written to Daniells asking for help. In Farnsworth's own words, quoted by Daniells in his letter to White:

" 'Brother Ballenger has got into a condition of mind which would seem to me to unfit him entirely to preach the message. He has been studying the subject of the sanctuary a good deal lately, and he comes to the conclusion . . . that when He [Christ] ascended He went immediately into the Most Holy Place and that His ministry has been carried on there ever since. He takes such texts as Hebrews 6:19 and compares them with twenty-five or thirty expressions of the same character in the Old Testament where he claims that in every instance the term "within the veil" signifies the Most Holy Place. . . .

"'He sees clearly that his view cannot be made to harmonize with the testimonies, at least he admits freely that he is totally unable to do so, and even in his own mind . . . there is an irreconcilable difference.'"[2]

Thus the problem had been relayed to the General Conference president by Farnsworth, a man who had been baptized in the dead of winter at Washington, New Hampshire, in a hole cut through two feet of lake ice, and who had no intention of becoming confused over something as basic as the sanctuary. And Daniells, having digested this and a great deal more, was writing to Elder White, wondering aloud how the denomination ought to handle the problem. "I shall be glad to have him get out of Great Britain," he mused, "but what we can do with him here is more than I can say at present. . . . It seems strange that a man who has been in this message all his life should get switched off on such a question. The sanctuary is the central pillar of this whole movement; you remove that, and everything tumbles.

"Do you know this brother, and have you any counsel to give?"[3]

Indeed, Elder White did know Albion Ballenger, and so for that matter did Ellen White. He was a handsome man, with a huge, flowing mustache and a charisma that could sweep many people with him, and this was not his first misadventure at tampering with basic articles of faith. A few years before, while assistant editor of the Adventist religious liberty magazine, he had gotten the idea that the church ought to make itself more appealing by deemphasizing distinctive doctrines such as the Sabbath. The result had been a vision that Ellen White had received while at Salamanca, New York, and that she finally revealed under the most impressive circumstances. (Repeatedly she tried to relate the vision, but each time it vanished from her recollection; only later was she able to recount it—the very *day* after Ballenger's remarks in a committee meeting.) Ballenger had heeded the divine message on that occasion, confessing in tears that he had been wrong. But now a whole new problem was brewing, and he was brought home from England while the brethren wondered exactly what to do with him.

Ellen White had little doubt. In mid-May of 1905 she attended the General Conference session in Takoma Park. While walking down the hallway of the college dormitory serving as guest quarters, she chanced to see Ballenger, and she had a pointed message to deliver. "You are the one whom the Lord presented before me in Salamanca," she declared, and then she went on to say some things that can only be deduced from her diary. "And now again our Brother Ballenger is presenting theories that cannot be substantiated by the Word of God. . . . I declare in the name of the Lord that the most dangerous heresies are seeking to find entrance among us as a people, and Elder Ballenger is making spoil of his own soul. . . .

"Your theories, which have multitudes of fine threads, and need so many explanations, are not truth, and are not to be brought to the flock of God. . . . God forbids your course of action—making the blessed Scriptures, by grouping them in your way, to testify to build up a falsehood.

"Let us all cling to the established truth of the sanctuary."[4]

Ballenger's response was to meet with a committee of twenty-five denominational leaders, from which evolved a document he called "The Nine Theses." Adventist beliefs regarding the sanctuary were wrong in "almost every cardinal point," he asserted, and he particularly argued against applying the first-apartment ministry to the period after Christ's ascension.[5] If one followed Ballenger's reasoning, the 2300-day prophecy collapsed, the 1844 message went with it, the investigative judgment suddenly became a theological embarrassment that had to be explained away. As A. G. Daniells had put it so aptly, "everything tumbles"; and no one saw that more clearly than Ellen White.

"In clear, plain language I am to say to those in attendance at this conference that Brother Ballenger has been allowing his mind to receive and believe specious error," she said just a few days later. "This message, if accepted, would undermine the pillars of our faith." And then she referred pointedly to the seventh chapter of Matthew: "Beware of false prophets, which come to you in sheep's clothing, but inwardly they are ravening wolves." [6]

"Those who try to bring in theories that would remove the pillars of our faith concerning the sanctuary or concerning the personality of God or of Christ, are working as blind men," she continued. "They are seeking to bring in uncertainties, and to set the people of God adrift, without an anchor. . . .

"Our Instructor spoke words to Elder Ballenger: 'You are bringing in confusion and perplexity by your interpretation of the Scriptures. You think that you have been given new light, but your light will become darkness to those who receive it. . . .

" 'Stop right where you are; for God has not given you this message to bear to the people.' " [7]

There was a danger here far larger than one man's confusion over basic Adventism. Albion Ballenger was an extremely persuasive person, a likable, nice-appearing man who occasionally wrote poetry and who spoke with such disarming sweetness that to disbelieve him seemed almost like repudiating one's own senses. For many people the whole thing seemed to come down to one simple question: How could Elder Ballenger be wrong?

There is admittedly a certain risk involved in dallying over the arguments of a man whom the divine messenger has said to be believing "specious error," but perhaps for one brief moment that risk is justified for the sake of getting an idea of the persuasive power Adventists had to face in 1905. Writing to Mrs. White, Ballenger suggested that he had to choose between believing her or believing the Bible, and he closed as follows:

"When side by side we stand before the great white throne; if the Master should ask me why I taught that 'within the veil' was in the first apartment of the sanctuary, what shall I answer? Shall I say, 'Because Sister White, who claimed to be commissioned to interpret the Scriptures for me, told me that this was the true interpretation, and that if I did not accept it and teach it I would rest under Your condemnation'?

"Oh, Sister White, that this answer might be pleasing unto the Lord. Then would I surrender to your testimony. Then would you speak words of encouragement to me again. Then would my brethren, with whom I have held sweet counsel, no longer shun me as a leper. Then would I appear again in the great congregation, and we would weep and pray and praise together as before." [8]

Ballenger had a powerful command both of words and emotions, and he clearly understood that people will instinctively support the underdog, sometimes even in the face of religious truth. That in itself was striking, because the very same tactic was being used by John Harvey Kellogg, who after sweeping the Battle Creek Sanitarium out of the church could still speak persuasively about getting "down on his face and weeping" over the injustices supposedly done him by Elder Daniells and Willie White. Canright too had affected a bit of martyrdom on leaving the Adventist faith, and Ballenger's use of the same technique would soon be evident in the title of his book *Cast Out for the Cross of Christ*. Interestingly, the men who left the church over this issue generally repeated a similar pattern: they would solemnly promise to cause no trouble for the church, only to commence an intense attack on

Adventism soon after leaving. Ballenger would be no different, and his apparently sweet letter to Ellen White reads quite the opposite when placed alongside some of the strident language in *The Gathering Call,* a paper in which he and his brother trumpeted anti-Adventist material from his headquarters near the denomination's vital new medical school.

But that remained to be seen only in the future. In 1905 individual Adventists could not know how far Albion Ballenger would go, for he probably did not know it yet himself; and in the meantime there was more than a passing danger that his personality and his gift for words might sweep a number of well-meaning people out with him. For one thing, he was acting more and more like a zealot, a man convinced that he had "new light" and who was more concerned about spreading his views than about anything else, including the welfare of the organized church. For another, he had accumulated an impressive array of scriptures with which to argue his points, and if one had not studied the issues personally, the mass of argument might be intimidating. "Already Elder Ballenger has mystified minds with his large array of texts," Ellen White noted in her diary late in 1905. "These texts are true, but he has placed them where they do not belong." [9]

"We have had to meet many men who have come with just such interpretations," she added, "seeking to establish false theories, and unsettling the minds of many by their readiness to talk, and by their great array of texts, which they have misapplied to suit their own ideas. *It is too late in this earth's history to get up something new.*" [10]

If that had been the only danger, the church would have had plenty to think about. But there was more. There was another jeopardy, one so unimaginably huge that it could be seen only through eyes that had glimpsed the invisible world. And now Ellen White pulled back the curtain to give the church a startling view of the unseen: *In 1905, heresy was being presented by more than men; it was also being presented by fallen angels.*

To understand what Ellen White was about to tell the church, one has to understand the deep, literal reality of the world she often experienced, just beyond the realm of mortal sight. For her, celestial beings were no mere abstraction; they were a reality, often seen, sometimes struggling intensely over the fate of a human soul. They lived and sang and sometimes wept, and watched with deepest interest to see whether the church would really live the Advent message. They came and went continually from earth to heaven, presenting a golden card at heaven's portal as they entered the realm of light. And there were other angels, driven by a compulsion to evil so monstrous that it is incomprehensible to ordinary mortals, demon angels bound for destruction and determined to drag every last being on earth down with them if there were a chance of doing so. Again and again Ellen White had pointed God's people to the reality of this great struggle, to the necessity of doing nothing that would give evil forces any leverage on the soul. "If you could see the pure angels with their bright, searching eyes intently fixed on you, watching to record how the Christian glorifies his Master; or could you observe the exulting, sneering triumph of the evil angels, as they trace out every crooked way, and then quote Scripture which is violated, and compare the life with this Scripture which you profess to follow but from which you swerve, you would be astonished and alarmed for yourselves," she had written in 1868.[11] In 1899 she had described a "great conflict going on between invisible agencies, the controversy between loyal and disloyal angels. Evil angels are constantly at work, planning their line of attack. . . . Pray, my brethren, pray as you have never prayed before. We are not prepared for the Lord's coming."[12]

Now the year was 1905. John Harvey Kellogg was in the process of leaving the church, taking with him its largest institution and the flower of its minds; Albion Ballenger was proclaiming "new light" on the sanctuary, leaving in his wake divided churches and Adventists no longer clear on the major pillars of their faith. Everywhere the forces of evil seemed to be on the march, swallowing territory like a pillaging army, and perhaps a hint of the reason can be found in the diary of Ellen White, written on the last day of October: "Satan is using all his science in playing the game of life for human souls. *His angels are mingling with men, and instructing them in the mysteries of evil. These fallen angels will draw away disciples after them, will talk with men, and will set forth principles that are as false as can be, leading souls into paths of deception.* These angels are to be found all over the world, presenting the wonderful things that will soon appear in a more decided light. God calls upon His people to gain an understanding of the mystery of godliness." [13]

So *that* was it. In addition to human enemies, Satan was calling in fallen beings from the world of darkness. Unwittingly, and in the name of new truth, human beings were allying with the powers of evil, and Ellen White described the process in terms calculated to drive people to their Bibles, and to their knees: "False theories will be mingled with every phase of experience, and advocated with satanic earnestness in order to captivate the mind of every soul who is not rooted and grounded in a full knowledge of the sacred principles of the Word." [14]

Apparently, powerful psychological mechanisms would be employed, calculated to draw people toward the charisma of human personalities and thus to make the new teachings all the more appealing. "In the very midst of us all arise false teachers, giving heed to seducing spirits whose doctrines are of satanic origin. These teachers will draw away disciples after themselves. Creeping in unawares, they will use flattering words and make skillful misrepresentations with seductive tact." [15]

People would be drawn into an error so powerful that "when they once accept the bait, it seems impossible to break the spell that Satan casts over them."[16] Those who were thus entrapped would have no idea of their true condition; they would "protest at the thought that they are ensnared, and yet it is the truth."[17]

In a word, astonishing. It was almost beyond explanation. People who had enjoyed the greatest religious light in history were now imperiled by errors that could leave them trapped and they would not even know it. For nearly two thousand years Christians had soberly intoned the Biblical warning about errors so subtle as to deceive, if possible, the very elect. Like Peter, generation after generation of believers had solemnly informed the Lord that this might happen to others, but never to them—yet now it was here, and Ellen White poured out word pictures of a great apostasy: "Many a star that we have admired for its brilliancy will then go out in darkness. Chaff like a cloud will be borne away on the wind, even from places where we see only floors of rich wheat."[18]

"What, I ask, can be the end?" she cried out on October 30, 1905. "Again and again I have asked this, and I have always received the same instruction: never leave a soul unwarned."[19]

"Never leave a soul unwarned." In the midst of its deepest challenges, the church was to fight back, never missing an opportunity to deliver the truth, to warn every last soul who would stand still long enough to listen. For now the war was in deadly earnest. God's work was being challenged by something Ellen White called the "alpha of deadly heresies."[20] And then she added an afterthought. This would not be the last such attack. Another would come, another even more treacherous for the work of God.

The alpha had arrived. The omega would surely come. And Ellen White "trembled for our people."[21]

Chapter 5

Omega

Ω "WHAT has been will be again, what has been done will be done again; there is nothing new under the sun." [1]

It has been said that those who fail to learn from history are condemned to repeat its mistakes. For Seventh-day Adventists that statement is more than a cliché. It is a certainty.

"Be not deceived; many will depart from the faith, giving heed to seducing spirits and doctrines of devils. We have now before us the alpha of this danger. *The omega will be of a most startling nature.*" [2]

That statement was made in July, 1904, as the denomination faced an array of troubles almost beyond imagining. Loss of its largest institution and the crippling of the vital medical work. Large-scale apostasy among some of its most influential men. Heresies so subtle that their implications went unrecognized even by those who urged them. Legal manipulations that poured wealth into some areas while the world field struggled to survive. And the forthcoming attack by Ballenger, striking at the very rationale for Adventism. It was a time when all the energies of every loyal member of the church were needed to keep the ship afloat, and yet in the midst of the crisis Ellen White took time to warn the church about a danger still in the future.

"In the book *Living Temple* there is presented the alpha of deadly heresies," she said. "The omega will follow, *and will be received by those who are not willing to heed the warning God has given."* [3]

Omega. Something else would come, sufficiently similar to the present crisis to justify linking the two events by letters taken from a common alphabet. Beyond that, God's servant said very little. It was a cryptic warning, shouted into the wind of an engulfing crisis almost as an aside, a gift to the future given at a moment when she had almost no time for anything but the present. Yet Ellen White left some clues as to what the omega might involve, and from the urgency of her warning it appears essential that we try to piece them together.

From the Spirit of Prophecy we can know at least three things for certain about the omega. It was not a part of the alpha apostasy; it would "follow" later. It would be even more deadly than the alpha, so terrible a challenge that Ellen White "trembled" for our people. And it "will be received by those who are not willing to heed the warning God has given." In other words, those who choose to follow the counsel of God only when it suits their personal preferences apparently will be easy targets of opportunity for the omega deception.

But if we probe Ellen White's choice of symbolism, there seems to be even more that we can decipher. In 1904 she sees that something fearful is happening to the church. Doors that once stood open to the gospel are swinging shut. Even the most basic truths are being questioned in every way. It is a dreadful experience that she openly fears may cost her her life, and looking into the future, she sees that it will happen again, near the end of time. Somehow God's people must be warned, and Mrs. White reaches for a figure to describe two events, separated by time but similar in nature. In describing the great apostasy of the future, she does not use the next Greek letter after alpha. She does not warn about a "beta" apostasy or "gamma" or even "delta." Instead she plunges far ahead, to the end of the alphabet, and chooses a symbol that Christ has used in connection with the end. Alpha and omega.

The implications are clear. There are two events, separated but similar. One occurs at the end of time. And if you understand the first, you will recognize the second.

Of one thing we can be almost certain: the omega will attack basic doctrines of the Seventh-day Adventist Church. Almost every major apostasy has uniformly included three areas of attack: the sanctuary, the investigative judgment, and the Spirit of Prophecy—always in the name of great good for the church, cloaked in such terms as *reformation.* "The enemy of souls has sought to bring in the supposition that a great reformation was to take place among Seventh-day Adventists, and that this reformation would consist in giving up the doctrines which stand as the pillars of our faith, and engaging in a process of reorganization."[4] Such an apostasy, she warned, could have devastating effects, for Adventism is a system of highly interrelated truths; attack one, and dominoes begin to tumble. The "principles of truth" long believed by the remnant church "would be discarded." A "new organization" would be established. Books of a "new order" would be written. Intellectual philosophy would replace the fundamental truths of the church. The Sabbath would be "lightly regarded." And the new movement would be spearheaded by aggressive men who would allow "nothing . . . to stand in the way."[5]   1 SM 205

It was a chilling picture. Under the banner of "new light" powerful forces would seek to bend the church of God into some unrecognizable new shape. They would act in the name of reformation, forgetting that the reformation for which the Bible called was one of life, not of established doctrine; forgetting, too, Ellen White's warning that the church did not need new light nearly as badly as it needed to live up to the light it already had. And in the process they would thus almost certainly introduce deep confusion over one of the most basic issues in the church: How should Adventists live?

There is nothing subtle about Adventism. It does not whisper to the world, it cries out. It begins, in Bible imagery, as angels shout from midheaven. It ends with the mightiest earthquake in history. And having gotten the world's attention, it holds up the divine law and proclaims that the judgment has already begun. There is little room in such a religion for double standards, for preaching one thing and doing something else. God's people claim to be living in the great antitypical day of atonement, their lives passing in final review before God, and one of the greatest imaginable failures would be to give such a message and then live as if it were untrue.

Yet that is the invariable result of an attack on the sanctuary or the investigative judgment. Adventism produces an inevitable problem for every individual who has ever tried to rewrite Adventist truth. The sanctuary and sanctification are indivisibly connected. Attack one, and you also injure the other. Remove the sanctuary truth, with its powerful message of true reform, and you are soon left wandering in a maze of theological terms, trying to explain why works are even necessary. Attack sanctification, and you can never rest comfortably until you remove the haunting light of the sanctuary.

Is there a possibility that this too will be repeated as part of the omega? Perhaps. And one of the best insights can be found in the symbolism used by God's messenger. Remember that alpha and omega are two letters at the polar extremes of the same alphabet. They are linked by something in common, yet they look in opposite directions. There is a significance here that becomes apparent with a little reflection.

To grasp it, one has to look back at the theology of the alpha. Throughout his life Kellogg staunchly proclaimed his belief in Christianity. Viewed superficially, even the statements in his final interview with elders from the Battle Creek tabernacle sound like the words of a devout Christian. Yet Kellogg's theology, taken to its logical end, removes the need for a Saviour. God, he claimed, was in everything—in the air we breathe (in the form of the Holy Spirit), in the sunlight, even in the lawns that stretched outside his home. If God is in everything, He must also be in man; and thus every human act becomes an act of God. Divinity becomes so internal to man that the very thought of an external Saviour becomes meaningless.

No Saviour—nothing outside of man. That, taken to an extreme that neither Kellogg nor Waggoner may have ever fully realized, is the ultimate message of the alpha. Now follow the logical symbolism of two letters, sharing the subject matter of a common alphabet but located at opposite extremes. If the alpha is in error regarding the role of Christ in salvation, and if it points in one direction in the Greek alphabet, is it possible that the omega will also misinterpret the work of Christ while pointing opposite? To put it another way, is there a possibility that the omega of "deadly heresies" will try to put Christ totally *outside* of man, thus introducing confusion over sanctification because it makes salvation totally *external*?

It is a question that deserves the most serious reflection. The role and work of Christ are the central truths of Christianity. Become confused about Christ's work, whether in the heavenly sanctuary or in the life, and, as Daniells so aptly put it, "everything tumbles." In 1904 Adventists were asked to believe a new doctrine that made salvation entirely internal. It was an enormously appealing error, perfectly designed to attract people in an age of optimism in which everyone from financiers to ministers talked about human advancement.

But what about a later age, in which a disillusioned world looks back across the wreckage of its century and sees only endless war and great depression and lights fading out beneath a sky unfit to breathe? What about Adventists, weary and discouraged, ripe for something that seems to offer an easier way out of the endless challenge? To that group of people the devil could never hope to sell the boundless optimism of the alpha. But he could do something else. In a world turned upside down he could turn the alpha upside down. He could take the same subject and approach it from the opposite extreme. He could reach for the end of the alphabet and find omega. And his words, falling across a weary church, might sound like music: "Relax; the work is done and has been for centuries. Your only task is to believe that."

And in one stroke the master deceiver would have taken Adventism back in time to a point before its beginning, erasing God's movement like some strange time warp out of science fiction. For Adventism's unique gift to the world is its sense of urgency, a certainty of great events that require great preparation. At the very moment of its birth Adventism produced the most splendid exhibition of faith and works since Pentecost. The believers had taken the word *faith* beyond the dizziest summit that Luther ever dreamed of reaching; they had not only believed in Christ, they had expected to *see* Him, and the prospect of that event became more real to them than life on earth. Soon, they believed, they would look on His face, live with angels, witness to unfallen worlds. One did not approach that sort of prospect in careless indifference about his quality of life. "We are preparing to meet Him who, escorted by a retinue of holy angels, is to appear in the clouds of heaven to give the faithful and the just the finishing touch of immortality,"[6] Ellen White had written, and her words captured perfectly the urgency of 1844. It was a solemn time, an example of what it is *really* like to believe that Jesus is coming. Old wrongs were righted. "Many sought the Lord with repentance and humiliation. The affections that had so long clung to earthly things they now fixed upon heaven. . . .

"The barriers of pride and reserve were swept away. Heartfelt confessions were made, and the members of the household labored for the salvation of those who were nearest and dearest. Often was heard the sound of earnest intercession." [7] And the result? A power for witnessing thereafter imitated but seldom attained: "Vast crowds listened in breathless silence to the solemn words. Heaven and earth seemed to approach each other. . . . None who attended those meetings can ever forget those scenes of deepest interest." [8]

Had the church of God continued in that way, there would have been nothing it couldn't have done—the devil had to find a way to blunt that message. And it mattered little to him whether the people of God erred by thinking salvation was entirely internal, or whether they gave up, at last, beneath the gathering storm clouds of the end of time, relying on something that masqueraded as faith and ended in failure. For him there was only one necessity: he had to lead God's people away from the divine plan.

It was a situation remarkably similar to that faced by Israel at the Jordan. When obedient to God, they were invincible. There was no way King Balak could stop them, not even by hiring a prophet who helplessly intoned blessings over the nation he was bribed to curse. *And yet there was a way.* God's people could be conquered if they quit *acting* like His people. Balaam was powerless to curse Israel, but he could still bring them to the brink of disaster with a subtle scheme that led them outside the protection of God's law. God's blessings were free, but they could be forfeited.

So it was with Adventism. God's church was now standing at the Jordan—springtime's Jordan, flooded and swollen as it rushed toward the Dead Sea, a symbol of an angry world through which His people would have to pass on their journey home. There was no human way across that angry river, yet they could make the crossing—safe beneath the ark of God, which held His law. That was the unique message of Adventism. Great changes were coming; the world was headed toward its final events, and there was nothing more important than getting ready. No religious group in modern history had ever made the claims that Adventists made: claims of great new insights into the very structure of heaven, where Jesus was judging the world by a standard called the law of God. The whole reason for Adventism was found in that message. Before the world the believers had lifted the ark and edged toward the Jordan, and the most unthinkable of all calamities was that they might somehow, here on the brink, stumble and let it drop.

That was the issue, and there Satan chose to make his attacks on the church, just as Ellen White had said he would. Attacks on Adventism always seemed to involve its unique doctrines, striking at God's high standards for His people—either by saying that the requirements were unnecessary or by saying that they were unattainable. Here Canright had foundered, openly challenging the law, the Sabbath, the inspiration of the Spirit of Prophecy. John Kellogg, approaching the same reef from another direction, had also made shipwreck of his faith with unproved ideas that wiped out the investigative judgment and put God's sanctuary inside the human body. Ballenger, Waggoner, Jones, McCoy, Conradi—all followed similar routes, running aground where they thought they saw a clear channel of truth. And as they did so, they would unwittingly demonstrate the role of works in Adventism.

The behavior of those who advocated the alpha provides some fascinating insights into the effects of false doctrine and gives some extremely useful signals for recognizing it when it reappears. Christ Himself had said that heresy can sometimes be extremely difficult to detect, particularly when it is skillfully adapted to meet the mood of its era. At the end of time, there would appear errors capable of

deceiving the "very elect," a prophecy fulfilled with
sad accuracy in the alpha, which took out many of
Adventism's intellectual elite. And so God wisely
gave a second means by which truth and error can
be detected: fruits. Human behavior. The *means* by
which people go about promoting the things that are
important to them. And the means used by the
"reformers" of 1905 read like a checklist of warning
signals for which to watch in the final deception
called omega. At the head of the list is the same
tactic Lucifer used to introduce humanity to the
nightmare of sin. It is called dishonesty.

"The contest will wax more and more fierce,"
Ellen White warned in 1898. "Mind will be arrayed
against mind, plans against plans, principles of
heavenly origin against principles of Satan." And
then she foretold the tactics some would use.
"There are men who teach the truth, but who are not
perfecting their ways before God, *who are trying to
conceal their defections, and encourage an estrange-
ment from God.*" [9]

"In the very midst of us will arise false teachers,
giving heed to seducing spirits whose doctrines are
of satanic origin. These teachers will draw away
disciples after themselves. *Creeping in unawares,
they will use flattering words and make skillful
misrepresentations with seductive tact.*" [10] In almost
the same breath she said that "false theories will be
mingled with every phase of experience, and advocated with *satanic earnestness* in order to captivate
the mind of every soul who is not rooted and
grounded in a full knowledge of the sacred principles of the Word." [11]

Those predictions had come tragically true in
the case of Dr. Kellogg and the close circle of
followers who supported his maneuverings at Battle Creek. Deeply laid plots were put in motion that
for a time went unknown to anyone except the
conspirators—and the messenger of God, who saw
their meetings in visions of the night. By 1905 their
plans had nearly reached maturity; Battle Creek

Sanitarium had only a short time left as a Seventh-day Adventist institution, and Ellen White trumpeted an alarm to the church. "I wish to sound a note of warning to our people nigh and afar off. An effort is being made by those at the head of the medical work in Battle Creek to get control of property over which, in the sight of the heavenly courts, they have no rightful control. . . . *There is a deceptive working going on to obtain property in an underhand way.* This is condemned by the law of God. I will mention no names. But there are doctors and ministers who have been influenced by the hypnotism exercised by the father of lies. Notwithstanding the warnings given, Satan's sophistries are being accepted now just as they were accepted in the heavenly courts." [12] Earlier she had written a touching letter to her son, who faced the fury of the Michigan apostasy. "The doctor is endeavoring to bind medical institutions fast in accordance with his words, *as Satan worked in the heavenly courts to bind up the angels who he induced to unite with his party to work to create rebellion in heaven.*" And then she had added, "I am sorry for you, Willie. I wish not to be in Battle Creek. But stand stiffly for the truth." [13]

The same tactics now spread to other areas. Kellogg and his co-workers, exposed by God's messenger, turned their attacks on her. Subtle doubts were cast on the reliability of her messages, often by workers who for tactical or employment reasons pretended to be giving their support. (Kellogg could keep people spellbound as he flooded them with stories about how he had "set a trap for Sister White," and how her testimonies to him were fueled by misinformation provided by A. G. Daniells and "Weeping Willie" White.) All of this Ellen White saw and described with dispassionate accuracy. "Very adroitly some have been working to make of no effect the Testimonies of warning and reproof that have stood the test for half a century. *At the same time, they deny doing any such thing.*" [14]

Truth. The most vital commodity in the world. Our very survival depends upon it. Each day we utterly rely on accurate information about even the simplest things such as the color of a traffic signal or the load-bearing capacity of a beam. Without truth there is no safety, either in a physical or a spiritual sense. It is the only channel through which God communicates; *and truth was being manipulated by men who claimed to have a reformation message for the church of God,* men who were not even being honest about their true intentions.

"Before the development of recent events, the course that would be pursued by Dr. Kellogg and his associates was plainly outlined before me. He with others planned how they might gain the sympathies of the people. *They would seek to give the impression that they believed all points of our faith, and had confidence in the Testimonies. Thus many would be deceived, and would take their stand with those who had departed from the faith.*" [15]

All of which leads to another characteristic of the alpha, one about which God's people at the end of time need to be particularly forewarned. That tactic is the skilled manipulation of people. The leaders of the alpha had become so committed to changing the church that they seem to have decided that the ends justified the means. Conscious plans were set forth to misrepresent themselves as loyal Adventists who believed the truth but who had new light that, if Sister White could get a clear picture of it, she herself would adopt. Even such men as Dr. David Paulson, beguiled for a time by Kellogg, honestly thought that the new theology was supported by Ellen White's writings, an error that, she warned, Kellogg was trying hard to promulgate.[16] It was a masterfully executed deception, and the result was a core of bright, influential people who gathered around a man and a new movement, even if that meant leaving the church.

This has profound importance for people watching to identify the omega. God's truths are so interwoven, so tightly logical, that to become diverted from them almost always involves a distracting stimulus such as a charismatic individual. There is a powerful human tendency to follow strong leadership, particularly if that leader sparkles with charisma. Whole nations—millions of people—have done exactly that, following a man down into the shadows where the rays of the sun cannot reach. It is a threat from which even God's people are not immune. Ellen White warns that there is a class particularly vulnerable to this tactic. "There are many who have not perfected a Christian character; their lives have not been made pure and undefiled through the sanctification of the truth; and they will bring their imperfections into the church, and deny their faith, *picking up strange* *theories, which they will advance as truth.*"[17] (There is a point here that ought to be explored for a moment. If a false leader once senses this, realizes that imperfections in the lives of his followers bind them more closely to him and his theories, there will be a powerful motivation for him to devise a theology that leaves people comfortable with their errors.)

"Brilliant, sparkling ideas often flash from a mind that is influenced by the great deceiver. Those who listen and acquiesce will become charmed, as Eve was charmed by the serpent's words. They cannot listen to charming philosophical speculations, and at the same time keep the word of the living God clearly in mind."[18]

One night in 1904, before leaving Washington for Berrien Springs, Ellen White was shown a meeting in progress in Battle Creek. "[Dr. Kellogg] was speaking, and he was filled with enthusiasm regarding his subject.... *In his presentations he cloaked the matter somewhat,* but in reality he was presenting... scientific theories which are akin to pantheism.

"After looking upon the pleased, interested countenances of those who were listening, One by my side told me that the evil angels had taken captive the mind of the speaker." And Ellen White added that she was "astonished to see with what enthusiasm the sophistries and deceptive theories were received." [19]

There was a danger in even discussing such matters with leaders of the alpha, and it again involved basic honesty. "When engaged in discussion over these theories, their advocates will take words spoken to oppose them, and will make them appear to mean the very opposite of that which the speaker intended them to mean." [20] In other words, even to talk with these men was to run the risk of being misquoted, of having one's words twisted so that they appeared to support Kellogg's ideas. Thus the conspirators of the alpha could make it appear that multitudes were "with them," and that their following was much larger than it really was. . . . A deadly game, played by unorthodox rules that God's leaders couldn't use—a game played for human minds, like pawns on a chessboard, with the ultimate stakes being control of the church. One thing can be said with certainty: the game of the alpha was played in earnest and with eternal consequences.

To accomplish their persuasive goals, Kellogg and his followers used some fascinating psychological mechanisms. Meetings were often held at night, and at times into the early hours of the morning, when the listeners were weary and less able to think for themselves. "The long night interviews which Dr. Kellogg holds are one of his most effective means of gaining his point. His constant stream of talk confuses the minds of those he is seeking to influence. He misstates and misquotes words, and places those who argue with him in so false a light that their powers of discernment are benumbed. He takes their words, and gives them an impress which make them seem to mean exactly the opposite of what they said." [21] Ellen White wrote him in anguish, reminding him that the same tactics had been used before, and had caused the fall of one third of heaven's angels. Lucifer, too, had skillfully used the technique of going from angel to angel, drawing them to make statements that he then repeated and misconstrued to other angels. It was a devastating tactic that made him seem to have more support than really existed, while at the same time it was used to discredit those loyal to God, weakening their credibility and hence their influence on the side of truth. It was a tactic against which even God had no effective countermeasure except time—and the certainty that one day Lucifer would go too far and blunder outside the veneer that masked his real character.

The technique of gossip seems to have been a part of the alpha, and is a danger for which God's church ought particularly to be on the lookout. "Even in our day there . . . will continue to be entire families who have once rejoiced in the truth, but who will lose faith because of calumnies and falsehoods brought to them in regard to those whom they have loved and with whom they have had sweet counsel." Their mistake was in listening. "They opened their hearts to the sowing of tares; the tares sprang up among the wheat . . . and the precious truth lost its power to them." For a time, Evelike, their excursion into this new game of gossip and false theology brought a strange sense of exhilaration: "False zeal accompanied their new theories, which hardened their hearts against the advocates of truth as did the Jews against Christ." [22]

So charisma, the skillful use of untruths about people on the side of right, and the appeal to follow personalities, all were large factors in an apostasy that swept out of the church even men who had once given the third angel's message "in verity." Every device was employed to draw loyalty to a man and to his tinseled ideas, and the technique worked with awesome success. It is a threat for which God's people ought to be watching with intense awareness to ensure that it does not happen again. And for those who feel drawn by the magnetism of a personality, who are intrigued by new ideas that may appeal even to leading thinkers, there is a warning out of 1905: "I am afraid of the men who have entered into the study of the science that Satan carried into the warfare in heaven. . . . When they once accept the bait, it seems impossible to break the spell that Satan casts over them." [23]

The point to remember is that the real issue was control of the church. If enough people could be converted to the new theology, if churches could send such "converts" to constituency meetings, if institutions could be packed with people committed to the alpha, the church would finally go that way, whether A. G. Daniells and Ellen White liked it or not. There is every reason to believe, from the writings of Ellen White, that well-structured and conscious efforts were being made to subvert the very organization of the church. Notice the choice of language in a warning given by her in June of 1905: *"I must warn all our churches to beware of men who are being sent out to do the work of spies in our conferences and churches—a work instigated by the father of falsehood and deception."* [24] Elsewhere she cautioned that "in the camp there have been many traitors in disguise, and Christ knows every one of them. God has been dishonored by disloyal subjects. . . . To those abiding in Battle Creek, I say, For your souls' sake, let as many as can, get away from its strife and its perils." [25]

The "strife" and "perils" to which she referred were becoming acute in 1906. As early as 1902 church members had threatened to sue the church to prevent the relocation of the Review and Herald Publishing Association to Washington, D.C. Now this spirit of strife and coercion surfaced again. The great Battle Creek tabernacle became the focal point of a struggle for control; a lawsuit was filed in the Michigan court to prevent transfer of the church property to the local Adventist conference. The loyal church members finally won, but only after a spectacular two-year fight. Even a Chicago newspaper trumpeted from beneath front-page headlines that the Adventist Church was about to be split "in twain," and laid much of the blame on Ellen White. The whole sorry affair served to illustrate another point of identity in the alpha: wherever it went, trouble followed.

The same thing had been seen in Ballenger's apostasy. Reporting from the British Isles, Elder Farnsworth had said that Ballenger " 'has been talking these things more or less until he said Brother Hutchinson in Ireland viewed the matter just as he did, and quite a number of influential lay brethren also. Brother Meredith who has charge of the work in Wales said that quite a number of the lay brethren in Wales were upset by this view, and in North England Brother Andross is having serious difficulty in the Birmingham church, and in other places too with some of the leading brethren on the subject of the sanctuary. . . . Somehow this dark cloud of apostasy made it hard for us.' "[26] And in Battle Creek, Kellogg had recently worked behind the scenes in a futile but troublesome effort to remove the General Conference leadership from office. There was a determined mood in all of this to change the church—by political process if possible, by subversion if necessary—and Ellen White's description is graphic: "Nothing would be allowed to stand in the way of the new movement."[27] There was a strange ruthlessness, seldom, if ever, seen before, in which longstanding friendships no longer seemed to count for much and traditional loyalties mysteriously disappeared. John Kellogg had been helped through medical school financially by the Whites: now he turned on his old friends with cutting attacks. A. T. Jones and E. J. Waggoner, who had traveled and preached with Ellen White, forsook old associations in favor of the new theology. Even Frank Belden, an Advent hymnwriter and nephew of Mrs. White, tried unsuccessfully to trick her into issuing a false testimony, and then filed suit against loyal members who were trying to protect church property. Everywhere the new theology went there seemed to be trouble, brought on by "mischievous tongues and acute minds, sharpened by long practice in evading the truth," which were "continually at work to bring in confusion, and to carry out plans instigated by the enemy." [28]

As we have seen before, another characteristic of the alpha was the manner in which it aggressively pursued the young people of the Adventist Church. After *The Living Temple* was printed, Kellogg sent it to local conferences and tried to enlist the youth in its distribution and sale. He also revived Battle Creek College, which put many students under the instruction of his brightest supporters. Taking them at an impressionable age, putting them into a classroom setting in which the instructor traditionally has high credibility, he hoped to gain a large following among the church's new generation. And thus the proponents of the new theology would have a strong second line of attack. If they did not succeed in pressing their viewpoint on the church, they need only wait, patiently train their students, and then scatter them through the world field so that the very structure of the organized work would begin to change imperceptibly. And one day the dissidents would have the influence and the votes, perhaps, to make the change official. In some ways, that may have been the most dangerous tactic of all. And on this point, Mrs. White was prepared to put everything, including her life, on the line. "God forbid that one word of encouragement should be spoken to call our youth to a place where they will be leavened by misrepresentations and falsehoods regarding the testimonies, and the work and character of the ministers of God.

"My message will become more and more pointed, as was the message of John the Baptist, even though it cost me my life. The people shall not be deceived." [29] The unkind remark is sometimes made that Ellen White was not attuned to the realities facing the church's young people. In 1904 she was ready to *die* for them.

Finally, those who were involved in the alpha apostasy had another point in common: they were adverse to the Spirit of Prophecy. Motivationally that is not difficult to understand; many of their fondest ideas ran headlong into firm opposition from Ellen White. Under the power of the Spirit of God their hidden plans were often brought to light, their meetings witnessed even from great distances. Not having divine truth on their side, they had to resort to some substitute, and the easiest expedient often seemed to be personal attacks on the messenger God had chosen to use. There was nothing new about that tactic; it can be seen as far back as Kadesh-barnea, where Israel—in full view of the divine cloud—blamed *Moses* for leading them through a difficult desert passage. And the result, then as later, was always separation from the blessings of God.

Chapter 6

"The Test Will Come to Every Soul"

IT WAS one o'clock in the morning, and Ellen White was sitting up, probably using a lapboard for a desk, writing as rapidly as her pen could move over the paper. She usually rose before dawn to do her work, but this morning, just an hour past midnight, she felt an urgency seldom before experienced. The people of God were headed for a great shaking, a great collision with error in which many would lose their way, and she was compelled to give them a last clear warning before it happened.

It had begun earlier that night with a vivid dream that she understood to be a divine message, and the story is best told in her own words:

"Shortly before I sent out the testimonies regarding the efforts of the enemy to undermine the foundation of our faith through the dissemination of seductive theories, I had read an incident about a ship in a fog meeting an iceberg. For several nights I slept but little. I seemed to be bowed down as a cart beneath sheaves. One night a scene was clearly presented before me. A vessel was upon the waters, in a heavy fog. Suddenly the lookout cried, 'Iceberg just ahead!' There, towering high above the ship, was a gigantic iceberg. An authoritative voice cried out, 'Meet it!' There was not a moment's hesitation. It was a time for instant action. The engineer put on full steam, and the man at the wheel steered the ship straight into the iceberg. With a crash she struck the ice. There was a fearful shock, and the iceberg broke into many pieces, falling with a noise like thunder to the deck.... Well I knew the meaning of this representation. I had my orders. I had heard the words, like a voice from our Captain, 'Meet it!' For the next few days I worked early and late, preparing for our people the instruction given me regarding the errors that were coming in among us." [1]

For some time Ellen White had been perplexed, wondering what to do about the spurious new ideas Kellogg was urging upon the church. For her, the greatest treasure on earth was God's church. Often it erred; many times she poured out earnest messages to its leadership, begging for reform. Yet never did her loyalty waver. And now it seemed that to meet a great challenge might provoke a split among the members of the church, resulting in a frightful loss of talent, means, and souls. It was a decision that was desperately hard for her to make.

For many months she had waited, hoping that something she said might touch a responsive chord in Kellogg's heart and still save him for the cause. But there was a signal, divinely appointed, by which she would know when the confrontation could be delayed no longer. That would be "when the leaders in Battle Creek made an open raid on the Testimonies"—when the Spirit of Prophecy came under open attack. Then she said, "Brethren, we now face the issue. 'Meet it' with all the strength and power of God." The issue was joined; the church went out to engage the enemy, and in the words of Ellen White, drawing from the imagery of Gideon, "the pitchers were broken, and the light shone forth in clear rays." [2]

The idea of a great crisis, in which members are lost to the cause, is an incongruous and yet inevitable part of Adventism. Somewhere, sometime, there will be a great challenge that will shake the church. In that ordeal many will be lost, even among prominent thinkers. "The time is not far distant when the test will come to every soul.... Many a star that we have admired for its brilliancy will then go out in darkness. Chaff like a cloud will be borne away on the wind, even from places where we see only floors of rich wheat."[3] And the issue that causes this great upheaval will be false doctrine.

"When the shaking comes, *by the introduction of false theories*, these surface readers, anchored nowhere, are like shifting sand."[4] One's only hope in that time is to know God's will as revealed in His Sacred Writings. "The days are fast approaching when there will be great perplexity and confusion. Satan, clothed in angel robes, will deceive, if possible, the very elect. . . . Every wind of doctrine will be blowing. . . . Those who trusted to intellect, genius, or talent will not then stand at the head of rank and file. They did not keep pace with the light." And then she makes a statement that is filled with tragic overtones: "In the last solemn work few great men will be engaged."[5]

Lest the implications of all of this escape, let us recognize how comprehensive a tragedy is described here. Apparently some overpowering delusion will sweep against the church, taking with it everyone who is not absolutely grounded, no matter how highly educated. Jesus Himself warned of errors that, if it were possible, would "deceive the very elect." Paul foretold "grievous wolves" and warned that "of your own selves shall men arise, speaking perverse things, to draw away disciples after them."[6] It is not open error, not frontal attacks on the Christian faith that drag men out of the truth; it is rather a subtle mixture of truth and error, so cleverly combined that one's only hope of recognizing it is through the aid of the Holy Spirit and the diligent study of God's revealed truth. It will be necessary to deny even the apparent realities of one's senses, and walk by faith alone in the light that proceeds from God's Word.

There will be a great revival, we are told, just before the final visitation of God's judgments upon the earth. Knowing this in advance, Satan "will endeavor to prevent it by introducing a counterfeit. In those churches which he can bring under his deceptive power he will make it appear that God's special blessing is poured out; there will be manifest what is thought to be great religious interest. Multitudes will exult that God is working marvelously for them, *when the work is that of another spirit.*"[7]

For generations we have accustomed ourselves to assuming that all this takes place mainly outside the Adventist Church and that we, safely inside God's remnant, will watch it in interested but detached security. And that assumption may leave us puzzled as to how the very elect in our own midst could be threatened with deception. Is there a possibility that we have underrated the enemy, that the same delusion of a false revival may also present itself in the midst of Adventism, accompanied by all the sensory trappings that demand belief? If we answer that question in the negative, we are hard pressed to explain why some of our "brightest lights" will go out and will become our most formidable, articulate enemies. Men and women do not become *that* angry over petty intra-church issues. That level of anger is shown only when people convince themselves that the church has rejected some idea that they perceive as vital religious truth.

So the shaking, which we have long expected and dreaded, will involve doctrine and—if history and logic are correct—will probably include the church's rejection of what some people feel is vital "new light." (Remember that Ellen White clearly says the shaking will result from "the introduction of false theories.") That leaves us with an important question: What will be attacked?

It is a question that might be dismissed as purely speculative, except that we already have several answers. For one thing, we know that the Sabbath will be a doctrinal issue at the end of time. Could it become a point of controversy even within the church? Before we dismiss that as impossible, we must recognize that it has *already happened.* Canright, after attacking the sanctuary doctrine, next turned his attacks on the Sabbath and on the law. Kellogg, while at first professing to believe the Sabbath doctrine, gradually drifted away from it in a behavioral sense and labored diligently to get the sanitarium off a Sabbathkeeping operational plan. Sabbath recreation for patients became more and more secular. It is important to realize that the Sabbath can be assaulted in many ways, some obvious, some profoundly subtle. And it can be attacked indirectly, by striking at the foundation on which it rests. It is, after all, found in the law. If we adopt a theology that downgrades God's law—that says, for example, that it is impossible to keep those precepts—then we have attacked the law's components, of which the Sabbath is one. We are told that near the end of time some Adventists will be required to defend their Sabbath observance in a courtroom setting. It is difficult for the writer, as an attorney, to imagine any court taking an Adventist seriously who demands the right to worship on Saturday but who simultaneously admits that he cannot keep the law on which the Sabbath is based.

Next, we know for a certainty that a major attack will be made against the Spirit of Prophecy. "The very last deception of Satan will be to make of none effect the testimony of the Spirit of God."[8] That is an incredible fact; it is difficult to imagine people rejecting something that gives them priceless advance information about the tactics of an enemy who would rob them of eternal life. Yet it is a familiar paradox, repeated as often as history reveals messengers from God. It is relatively easy to read the writings of a prophet two thousand years removed, whose language is not in the idiom of your own day, and whose descriptions of sin may not be so painfully applicable to you; it is something very different to accept with grace the words of one who speaks to your very time. But few things could be more important than acceptance of that message.

If history teaches us anything, the omega will probably also involve some sort of confusion over the role of works and sanctification. We know that this has nearly always been involved in past apostasies, either by direct theological attack or by the behavior of those advocating change. Canright openly attacked the law. Those claiming to have holy flesh attacked it in a disguised way, claiming to believe while indulging in all sorts of wrongdoing done in the name of holiness. Kellogg's era saw notorious immorality among some believers. Whenever Adventists either directly or indirectly have become confused over their behavioral responsibilities, great harm has always resulted. And so it is vital for us to understand what some have portrayed as a paradox in Adventism: the duty to expend human effort in bringing to fruition a gospel that, most Protestants argue, is a free gift from God that shouldn't require such human input.

It is an apparently complex question that is remarkably easy to answer if one understands two principles of law called condition precedent and condition subsequent. A condition precedent is one that is imposed on a person before he or she receives property. In order for title to vest, the individual must *do* some specified act, after which the property belongs to that person. In a religious sense, this is a counterfeit of the true gospel—and it is the most common form of religion known to man. All paganism has its roots deep in this concept; taken to its extreme, it demands human sacrifices in order to bring people into favor with deity. In Christianity, the only condition precedent is faith—a faith so complete that it leads to the surrender of one's entire will to a loving God.

Condition subsequent is an apparently similar but operationally very different sort of rule. Here property is transferred outright, without the requirement of any prior act. But it, too, is transferred on conditions—conditions that operate *after* the transfer. A man might convey land to his neighbor, for example, upon condition that it never be used for the sale of alcoholic beverages; if the neighbor ever breaches that condition, the land reverts to the original grantor. And that is a striking example, in human law, of the operative mechanism for the plan of salvation. The gift is free; in no sense can the new owner be said to have "earned" it; yet by his abuse of the conditions under which it was granted, he can make himself unfit for the neighborhood and thus unable to continue as an owner.

The concept of righteous living is indelibly imprinted on the structure of Adventism. Adventists, after all, claim to have the last warning message for the world, a message that is delivered with far more power by behavior than it is by mere words. "Ye are the light of the world," Christ said. "Let your light so shine before men, that they may *see your good works,* and glorify your Father which is in heaven." [9] There is no rationale in Christ's theology for embarrassment over good works, or for confusion over whether one is responsible for the fruitage of a sanctified life. In His plan, godly living seems to be one of the major ways of preaching earth's last message of hope.

Yet that issue seems also to emerge as a key element in the final ordeal of God's church, which Adventists have come to know as the shaking. "Some may say it is exalting our own merits to expect favor from God through our good works. True, we cannot buy one victory with our good works; *yet we cannot be victors without them.* . . . In every religious crisis some fall under temptation. The shaking of God blows away multitudes like dry leaves." [10] Early in the Advent experience Ellen White had warned that "just as long as God has a church, He will have those who will cry aloud and spare not, who will be His instruments to reprove selfishness and sins," and she saw that "individuals would rise up against the plain testimonies." The result would be tragic but inevitable. "The shaking must soon take place to purify the church." [11]

Strange words from a woman who would spend a lifetime trying to hold together a church that meant more than life itself to her. Such an ordeal seems foreign to a church that has been conditioned to believe in the importance of unity. It was hard for Ellen White; it will be hard for us. Yet even the gift of unity—like God's other gifts to man—can be abused. To introduce into the church errors that will destroy it, and then to protect them under the umbrella of "unity" is a problem that Ellen White had to address in 1904. "We are to unify," she declared, "but not on a platform of error." [12] "We are not to receive the words of those who come with a message that contradicts the special points of our faith. They gather together a mass of Scripture, and pile it as proof around their asserted theories. This has been done over and over again during the past fifty years." [13]

For Adventists who wished to avoid great danger, she had startling advice concerning the theories Dr. Kellogg promoted, which she herself finally had to employ in the doctor's case; don't even discuss them with those who, after the church has taken official action, persist on a course of their own. "At the time of the General Conference in Oakland, I was forbidden by the Lord to have any conversation with Dr. Kellogg. During that meeting a scene was presented to me, representing evil angels conversing with the doctor. . . . He seemed powerless to escape from the snare." [14] In 1907 she wrote a letter to be read in Oakland, Battle Creek, Chicago, and other large churches: "There is a spirit of wickedness at work in the church that is striving at every opportunity to make void the law of God. . . . The burden of our work now is not to labor for those who, although they have had abundant light and evidence, still continue on the unbelieving side." [15] To discuss these issues with those committed to error was to run the risk of being misquoted, she warned, and she cried out against those who "may gather up statements from my writings that happen to please them, and that agree with their human judgment, and, by separating these statements from their connection, and placing them beside human reasonings, make it appear that my writings uphold that which they condemn." [16]

And she especially warned about having such persons involved in Adventist schools. "Any man who seeks to present theories which would lead us from the light that has come to us on the ministration in the heavenly sanctuary, should not be accepted as a teacher." [17]

And so the standing orders for the church are clear, handed down as a legacy from pioneers in an earlier crisis, who drew the line at whatever cost to themselves and who, in the process, ensured that we would have preserved for our generation an ark of safety called the Seventh-day Adventist Church.

Chapter 7

Nine Salient Points

Q WE HAVE seen something called the alpha apostasy sweep across the Seventh-day Adventist Church at the turn of the century. We have watched it blunt the efforts of the church at the very time when God seems to have opened the world for the gospel. And we have heard the warning that something even more dangerous would come some-day. For that reason it is vitally important that we analyze what happened earlier and seek to recognize the signals that may herald the approach of the last great apostasy. Here, in summary, are the important points.

1. *Deception:* One of the major characteristics of the alpha was deceit. Sometimes outright untruths were told. Sometimes only part of the truth was given, and thus even truth could be made to give false impressions. Once Ellen White wrote to Dr. Kellogg advising him about a large building in Chicago. He often cited that testimony as proof that Ellen White was in error; no such building ever existed, he asserted smugly, and Sister White had simply been mistaken. What Dr. Kellogg did not bother to add was that his people at Battle Creek had fully *intended* to build it, proceeding so far as having a full set of architectural plans drawn, before the project got stopped.

Particularly did Mrs. White warn that some people would be dishonest about their belief in the Spirit of Prophecy and in the basic doctrines of the church. In vision she saw groups of people at Battle Creek counseling together and specifically planning to hide their antagonism to her writings and to certain fundamental beliefs. Thus concealing their true feelings, they felt they could more effectively appeal to Adventists who were basically loyal to the church and who would never listen to them if they disclosed their full intentions at the start. Again and again throughout the alpha one finds the truth being bent for the sake of some immediate goal. Perhaps Ellen White put it most graphically: "Mischievous tongues and acute minds, sharpened by long practice in evading the truth, are continually at work to bring in confusion."[1]

In the alpha, this technique also presented itself in the misuse of scriptures and Spirit of Prophecy writings. In 1905 Adventists were warned about people who "gather together a mass of Scripture, and pile it as proof around their asserted theories. ... And while the Scriptures are God's word, and are to be respected, the application of them, if such application moves one pillar from the foundation that God has sustained these fifty years, is a great mistake."[2]

Even more vivid is a warning she gave about future misuse of her own writings. "It will be found that those who bear false messages will not have a high sense of honor and integrity. *They will deceive the people, and mix up with their error the* Testimonies *of Sister White, and use her name to give influence to their work. They make such selections from the* Testimonies *as they think they can twist to support their positions, and place them in a setting of falsehood, so that their error may have weight and be accepted by the people.*"[3]

Interestingly, those engaging in misuse of truth may feel that they are absolutely right, and may act with a conviction that is impressive. Such was the case with Dr. Kellogg, and Mrs. White warned the General Conference leadership not to let him "beguile you by his statements. Some may be true;

some are not true. He may suppose that all his assertions are true; but you should neither think that they are, nor encourage him to believe that he is right."[4]

2. *Divisiveness:* The alpha disclosed the paradox of men claiming some wonderful new truth while at the same time dividing the church wherever their ideas were voiced. National boundaries seemed to have no effect on this splitting phenomenon. The Battle Creek tabernacle descended into turmoil. Churches in England, Scotland, and Wales also saw commotion when theories were advanced at variance from Adventist beliefs. Wisely, Christ has given His church the test of behavior by which the truth or falsity of new doctrine can be tested. Should the divisive elements of the alpha reappear in Adventism, history suggests that our people ought to be particularly wary.

3. *Attack on fundamental beliefs:* All major apostasies have shared the common ground of attacking the most basic Adventist beliefs, among which are the sanctuary, the investigative judgment, and the inspiration of the Spirit of Prophecy. At the turn of the century Ellen White could recall that over the past fifty years significant efforts had been made to subvert the fundamental truths of the church, particularly those of the sanctuary doctrine. To the student of history it is fascinating to watch this particular attack recur cyclically, each time with new fervor, as though it is being discovered for the first time. Often, advocates of change will use the rationale that even Ellen White urged receptivity to new light. They seldom add the *conditions* upon which she urged this: counsel with brethren of experience, and if the organized church does not see value in the idea, let it rest. And in no event will "new light" obliterate long-established fundamental truths. "Men and women will arise professing to have some new light or some new revelation, whose tendency is to unsettle faith in the old landmarks. ... False reports will be circulated, and some will be

taken in this snare. They will believe these rumors, and in their turn will repeat them. . . . Through this means many souls will be balanced in the wrong direction."[5] Elsewhere she included the sanctuary truth, the three angels' messages, the Sabbath, and the state of the dead as landmark doctrines, and warned that Satan would try to convince God's people that these need to be changed—something they should resist "with most determined zeal."[6]

4. *Covert attacks on the structure of the church:* One of the most startling charges ever made by Ellen White was that "spies" were at work, seeking to subvert even the basic structure of the church.[7] Conscious plans were laid to gain control of major institutions. Even conferences were threatened by this tactic, she said. In vision she witnessed secret meetings in which men planned how they could best gain control, win the sympathies of the people, and alter the structure of the church, and she described a conspiracy in which men were "linked together to support one another."[8] One can hope, but would be naive to assume, that such a threat will not be faced again. It is a particularly deadly threat to the work of God because it proceeds so quietly, spreading beneath the surface of an apparent calm until it is too late. If one is looking for indicia of the omega, this is a factor that cannot safely be ignored. And there are signs for which history tells us to look. Political struggles within a church or conference, as happened at Battle Creek. Evidence of well-organized movements at committee and constituency meetings that advocate ideas counter to the positions of the church. Widespread attacks against those who urge loyalty to the organized church and its teachings. Manipulation of institutional funds. (A famous book attacking the Spirit of Prophecy came out of the Battle Creek Sanitarium, written by doctors on its staff; funding for the project occurred under the most mysterious circumstances.) And perhaps the most disheartening sign of all, readily visible in the alpha: ministers, still on church

payroll, who may profess loyalty but whose actions tend to support movements at variance from the church. All are the visible signs of something very much larger. In a spectacular vision in 1904 Ellen White saw the church, symbolized as a ship, heading toward an iceberg. Only the tip of the iceberg could be seen, but it disclosed a danger that was deadliest below the waterline. The divine instruction was to "meet it"—hit it head-on. There would be a bone-jolting collision; everyone aboard would be shaken, *but the ship would remain afloat.* Hit the obstacle a glancing blow, and one would only open a gash into which the sea would flood uncontrollably. (In just eight years that very illustration would be lived out in the experience of the "unsinkable" *Titanic.*) The lesson in the symbol is crystal-clear: many of the dangers the church will face are hidden beneath the surface, disclosed only by a few indicia that are just the tip of a larger iceberg. These are the deadliest threats of all, and in Ellen White's vision they were met by hitting the obstacle head-on, with all the force the church could muster.

5. *Special efforts to attract the youth:* John Harvey Kellogg wrote a book in which he advanced ideas that could "sweep away the whole Christian economy."[9] He insisted on publishing it after Ellen White had warned against the subtleties of pantheism, after the General Conference had voted the project down, after the Review and Herald had burned to the ground. Upon publication he immediately courted the young people of the church, seeking them as allies in distributing his new theology. Every effort was made to reach the youth, including the reopening of Battle Creek College against divine counsel, preparation of special brochures aimed at young minds, and sending out representatives who actively recruited the youth for the Battle Creek venture. If he had been successful, the history of the Adventist Church might have been different. The appeal of spurious "new light" to the young is a special threat against

which modern Adventists need to guard, and for which fathers and mothers might do well to watch after rereading Ellen White's advice for parents of 1906.

"Parents, keep your children away from Battle Creek. . . . Specious heresy has been taking hold of minds, and its threads have been woven into the pattern of the figure. Who is responsible for giving young men and women an education that has left a seducing influence upon their minds? One father writes that of his two children who were sent to Battle Creek, one is now an infidel and the other has given up the truth.

"Letters such as this have been coming from different ones. The warning is given me to give to parents, If your children are in Battle Creek, call them away without delay." [10]

What was one of the primary causes of this crisis for young people in Battle Creek? The attitude, expressed by leading figures there, that the special messages of God to the Adventist Church were not reliable.

6. *Special attacks on the Spirit of Prophecy:* Few elements of the church draw so much fire during apostasy as does the Spirit of Prophecy. "The very last deception of Satan will be to make of none effect the testimony of the Spirit of God. . . . Satan will work ingeniously in different ways and through different agencies, to unsettle the confidence of God's remnant people in the true testimony." [11] Upon a little reflection it becomes apparent why this is so. Deception at the very end of time will be extremely powerful and subtle, and the promise is given that "all who believe that the Lord has spoken through Sister White, and has given her a message, will be safe from the many delusions that will come in these last days." [12] It would be astonishing if satanic power were not directed against this vital help for God's people. Sadly, he gains some of his strongest allies in the form of Adventists who depart the faith in search of something new, and who were

conditioned to do that by first rejecting the truth God had left in their path.

"Very adroitly some have been working to make of no effect the Testimonies of warning and reproof that have stood the test for half a century. At the same time, they deny doing any such thing." [13] Here is described a paradox. People are skillfully destroying the effectiveness of the Spirit of Prophecy while superficially claiming to believe it. Note that there is a difference between outright, open opposition, and subtle twists that make God's special messages of "no effect." We can be virtually certain that attacks on the Spirit of Prophecy, both directly and indirectly, will be part of the end-time omega apostasy. This is, after all, the "very last deception of Satan."

Therein lies a great potential for disaster among the people of God, for the messages to this church stand as a barrier between its people and many dangers. "One thing is certain: Those Seventh-day Adventists who take their stand under Satan's banner will first give up their faith in the warnings and reproofs contained in the Testimonies of God's Spirit." [14]

But it is an attack we can truly expect to see. "There will be a hatred kindled against the testimonies which is satanic. . . . Satan cannot have so clear a track to bring in his deceptions and bind up souls in his delusions if the warnings and reproofs and counsels of the Spirit of God are heeded." [15]

7. *A climate of personal attack:* Repeatedly in the alpha one sees authoritarian coercion on the part of those advocating the new teachings. Opposition to their ideas seems to have evoked a very personal reaction, to which they responded with personal attacks. In describing this unique feature of the apostasy, Mrs. White said that "nothing would be allowed to stand in the way of the new movement." [16] This is borne out as we recall the incident when the General Conference leader was threatened by a young worker avidly supporting the new theology.

That gentleman warned that if Elder Daniells did not line up, he would be turned out of office and "rolled in the dust." Many, including Kellogg and Ballenger, attacked Ellen White. Opposition to the alpha seemed to be the signal for an attack against anyone, including the highest levels of church leadership, who opposed it. That too is a type of behavior for which Adventists should be watchful as the omega approaches.

8. *Attacks on church standards:* The ideals of the Seventh-day Adventist Church have always been high, a behavioral message to the world that humanity will soon stand before a righteous God. Frequently those standards have been attacked by people who claim that Adventists are legalists trying to work their way to heaven. When that accusation comes from outside the church, most of God's people are able to recognize it for what it is. But what would be the effect of that attack should it ever come from *inside* the church? The Spirit of Prophecy has a sobering answer, *given in the very words of Lucifer as he counsels with his fallen angels on how best to destroy the Seventh-day Adventist Church:*

" "Through those that have a form of godliness but know not the power, we can gain many who would otherwise do us harm. Lovers of pleasure more than lovers of God will be our most effective helpers. Those of this class who are apt and intelligent will serve as decoys to draw others into our snares. Many will *not fear their influence, because they profess the same faith. We will thus lead them to conclude that the requirements of Christ are less strict than they once believed, and that by conformity to the world they would exert a greater influence with worldlings.* Thus they will separate from Christ; then they will have no strength to resist our power, and *erelong they will be ready to ridicule their former zeal and devotion.'* " [17]

9. *The claim of a reform message for the church:* There is terrible danger in misidentifying this point, for the Bible and the Spirit of Prophecy plainly indicate that there will be reform in God's

church; the problem is identifying the true and separating it from the false. Fortunately, there is an answer.

"The enemy of souls has sought to bring in the supposition that a great reformation was to take place among Seventh-day Adventists, and that this reformation would consist in giving up the doctrines which stand as the pillars of our faith." [18] The test, therefore, seems to be whether "reform" agrees with established truth (in which case it is the true reform that matters, reform of *life*) or whether it urges abandonment of old truths in favor of something new (in which case it is a spurious reform of *doctrine* rather than life). It may be that this is a danger against which Adventists ought especially to guard. They are a reform-minded people; their whole message urges reformation. And hence if the enemy comes to them through this avenue, there is a possibility they might be more easily deceived, simply because the "goal" of the new doctrine seems to be something everyone has always wanted. The discriminating test is simple: Does the new teaching urge reform of life, or change of established truth?

"Satan has laid every measure possible that nothing shall come among us as a people to reprove and rebuke us, and exhort us to put away our errors," Ellen White wrote, describing the need for true reform. "But there is a people who will bear the ark of God. Some will go out from among us who will bear the ark no longer. But these cannot make walls to obstruct the truth; for it will go onward and upward to the end." [19]

And therein lies the hope for God's church, even during the powerful challenges of the omega. Nowhere is assurance given that victory is *easy;* repeatedly the assurance is given that it is *possible.* "Those who are in harmony with God, and who through faith in Him receive strength to resist wrong and stand in defense of the right, will always have severe conflicts and will frequently have to stand almost alone. But precious victories will be theirs while they make God their dependence. His grace will be their strength. Their moral sensibility will be keen and clear, and their moral powers will be able to withstand wrong influences. Their integrity, like that of Moses, will be of the purest character." [20]

The omega: a mysterious danger that waits for the church at the end of time. Ellen White saw it and "trembled for our people." And she left behind for us a legacy of hope to carry into that great challenge.

"To stand in defense of truth and righteousness when the majority forsake us, to fight the battles of the Lord when champions are few—this will be our test." [21]

Chapter 8

"Like a Desolating Cyclone"

THE year was 1914. Across the city of Battle Creek, dusty-bright in the early-summer sun, only memories reminded of what had been—of what *might* have been. On the corner of Washington and Main there was little indication that the Review and Herald Publishing Company had ever stood there, that once this had been the location of the General Conference. Battle Creek College, reopened with such high hopes by Dr. Kellogg, was closed, a dismal failure. Adventists were comparatively few now, and old-timers could recall the forest of "For Sale" signs that had appeared as the colony broke up. "The world will know the reason," Ellen White had once warned, and now D. M. Canright published a new edition of his book *Seventh-day Adventism Renounced*—and unwittingly ensured the fulfill-ment of her prediction.

"Battle Creek, Michigan, furnishes a good illus-tration of the failure of Adventism after a fair trial. . . . When I withdrew in 1887, there were nearly two thousand Sabbathkeepers here, all united. Often I preached in the great tabernacle when every seat, below and in the gallery, was full. In the college I taught one class of about two hundred, all young men and women preparing to work either as ministers or Bible readers. Now, 1914, the college is closed and lost to the cause; the sanitarium has revolted from the denomination, and nearly all the management, doctors, nurses and helpers are Sunday keepers; the publishing houses were burned down and the remnant moved away; the church has dwindled down to about four or five hundred; the tabernacle is largely empty and an elephant on their hands. . . . Large numbers have backslidden, lost faith in everything, and attend nowhere. It has been like a desolating cyclone."[1]

Fourteen years had passed since that bright January morning at the dawn of a new century, when the world stood ready and the Advent message had a chance to go in the sunlight. Now the day was over, its last shadows about to be drawn tight by a 19-year-old Serbian nationalist with a pistol. In the Bosnian town of Sarajevo, a confused chauffeur made a wrong turn and drove his open limousine down a crowded street. Behind him, sheltered by a parasol from the intense summer sun, sat a royal couple whose life had been a classic love story and for whom this day was their fourteenth anniversary. For a moment the chauffeur hesitated, then tried to turn the car around, and as he did so, two shots rang out. Archduke Francis Ferdinand and his wife slumped in the seat; and the long day of opportunity was over. The first shots of World War I had been fired. From now on the church would have to work in a world descending into darkness.

So many lights had gone out. J. H. Kellogg, leader of the medical work, whose medical school expenses had been partly paid by James and Ellen White; Albion Ballenger, who had decided to redo the sanctuary truth using theological treatises rather than the Spirit of Prophecy; Elders A. T. Jones and E. J. Waggoner, who had traveled and preached with Ellen White; Elder George Tenney, editor, minister, missionary; Elder L. McCoy, chaplain of the Battle Creek Sanitarium—to which were added, Canright hastily pointed out, "many persons in important positions as business managers, college professors, doctors, etc. All these are now out of the church, and all their influence is against the body."[2] The loss had been staggering; and now, like the lingering coal smoke from the Review and Herald fire, it left a haunting question that hung over the church: How could such a thing happen? What could produce such a massive apostasy among the denomination's brightest minds?

The answer was disarmingly simple, and interestingly enough it was one that the church had had all along. In the still-peaceful days of 1898, Ellen White had clearly warned what could happen. "There never will be a time in the history of the church when God's worker can fold his hands and be at ease, saying, 'All is peace and safety.' Then it is that sudden destruction cometh. Everything may move forward amid apparent prosperity; but Satan is wide awake, and is studying and counseling with his evil angels another mode of attack where he can be successful. The contest will wax more and more fierce on the part of Satan. . . . *Mind will be arrayed against mind, plans against plans, principles of heavenly origin against principles of Satan. Truth in its varied phases will be in conflict with error in its ever-varying, increasing forms, and which, if possible, will deceive the very elect.*"[3] There, if one cared to think about it, was the whole history of the crisis, presented five years before Kellogg's book was ever published. Satan himself was directing this attack; the commander in chief of the forces of darkness had taken the field. The battle had been fought on a supernatural level, in which, without the special protection of supernatural help, even the brightest minds would be scattered like leaves before an autumn wind. Kellogg, Jones, Waggoner, McCoy—all had gone out to face the enemy after first deciding to substitute their own judgment for the warnings of God's messenger, and they had thus stripped themselves of the only defense that really mattered. Somewhere in the course of events they had become deadly sure that they were right, that it was time to escape from a "dead body of dead prophecies," and now as they scattered from Adventism they did so with pious prayers for God's blessing on their departure.

And across the valley of time echoed the words of Ellen White given back in 1903, words spoken before it was too late for most of them: "Satan has his allies in men. And *evil angels in human form will appear to men,* and present before them such glowing representations of what they will be able to do if they will only heed their suggestions, that often they change their penitence for defiance. . . . Sin has darkened the reasoning powers, and hell is triumphing. O, will not men cease to trust in human beings?"[4]

Evil angels in human form. There was no hope of surviving such a challenge in human strength. Humanity had no answer for the logic of an angel's mind, where memories of paradise twisted crazily into a deception so powerful that one third of heaven's forces had at first been unable to recognize it. No amount of education or experience equipped a man to face a trap like that, and John Kellogg, for one, had walked straight into it while bells rang and lights flashed from the pages of Ellen White's warning.

One night in the early summer of 1904 Ellen White had seen in vision a meeting going on in Battle Creek. A number of physicians and ministers were present, listening to Dr. Kellogg expound his ideas of God in everything, unaware that they were being supernaturally observed. Mrs. White particularly noted the "pleased, interested countenances of those who were listening," and then her heavenly Companion turned to her with a chilling message. "Evil angels had taken captive the mind of the speaker," He said. He went on to warn that "just as surely as the angels who fell were seduced and deceived by Satan, so surely was the speaker under the spiritualistic education of evil angels.

"I was astonished to see with what enthusiasm the sophistries and deceptive theories were received," Mrs. White recounted, pointing out that Kellogg, emboldened by his success in sweeping ministers and doctors with him, had then called a special council at Battle Creek to press his ideas further on the organized church.[5]

"You flatter yourselves that you are moving under the inspiration of divine advancement," Ellen White warned the people in Battle Creek, "but some are following the false inspiration that deceived the angels in the heavenly courts."[6] To Kellogg she addressed the warning that he was being "hypnotized" by Satan (something he derided as absurd). In October of 1905 she warned of "men who have entered into the study of the science that Satan carried into the warfare in heaven."[7] In the face of such warnings Kellogg and his followers had plunged ahead, their minds quieted by the doctor's assurances that Ellen White's testimonies were not always trustworthy. Thus they had arrived, at last, at a tragic fulfillment of another of her predictions: "If permitted, evil angels will work the minds of men until they have no mind or will of their own.... Thus it will be with physicians or ministers who continue to bind up with the one who has had light, who has had warnings, but who has not heeded them."[8]

The same sad lesson had been illustrated in the life of Albion Ballenger. One night during an evangelistic meeting in London he had attempted to present the subject of the sanctuary. Terribly discouraged by the way in which he had preached, he had vowed that he would "'never preach again until I know what I am preaching.'" And then he had made a fatal mistake. "'I am not going to get it from our books,'" he declared. "'If our brethren could obtain it from the original sources, why can't I?'" Elder Ballenger was making the same mistake already made by Dr. Kellogg: the assumption that nothing was really involved here except human reasoning, in which one man's research was just as good as another's. "'I will go to the books or commentaries and all these various sources from which Elder Uriah Smith obtained light on the subject,'" he announced, and so saying he promptly walked straight off into darkness. For the Adventist doctrine of the sanctuary was not to be found in "books or commentaries"—not to be found anywhere except from the same Source as was sought by that circle of praying men and women who had studied through the cold autumn nights of 1844, and in whose midst was the same special messenger who now warned Ballenger to turn around before it was too late. He too had chosen to ignore that plea, and he, like Kellogg, left the Adventist faith, never to return. In Riverside, California (just a few miles from the church's new medical school), he would spend his last sixteen years saying things about Ellen White that, beneath a veneer of apparent charity, worked to attack her credibility as a special messenger from God.[9]

"Like a desolating cyclone." Canright had meant the words for God's church, but how clearly they described the lives of those who left it. A whole galaxy of Adventist lights had gone out, each in its own way, each bound to the rest by the common tragedy of rejecting God's messenger at a time when fallen angels were walking the earth in human form. The church and the world were entering a new era. Now the mistake of stepping outside God's special protection could bring the most tragic and immediate results.

Nineteen fourteen. God's people have lived for fourteen years in the sunlight of earth's last summer day. Now the sky darkens with the first of autumn's storms. Across the vulnerable plains of Belgium comes the rumble of heavy artillery being moved, a sweeping cloud of dust, an endless line of gray uniforms that identifies General Karl von Bülow's Second Army. In Berlin exuberant troops parade for the last time down the brick streets; a young woman in a frilly white blouse breaks into their ranks, locks arms with a soldier, and marches with them. A few steps behind, a well-dressed businessman does the same, carrying a soldier's gun— smiling faces headed sightlessly into the terrible midnight of the Marne and Verdun, into a nightmare never seen before except by a little lady who, years before, had pleaded with her church for action. "Soon there will be death and destruction, increasing crime, and cruel, evil working against the rich who have exalted themselves against the poor. Those who are without God's protection will find no safety in any place or position. Human agents are being trained and are using their inventive power to put in operation the most powerful machinery to wound and to kill. . . . Let the means and the workers be scattered." [10]

Once there was sunlight, a golden moment filled with opportunity for the people of God, lost because a skillful enemy succeeded in diverting their attention from the only message they really had to give. And out of that tragedy emerges only one question that really matters: Will we let it happen again?

References

Prologue
  * Ellen G. White, *Testimonies for the Church* (Mountain View, Calif.: Pacific Press Pub. Assn., 1948), vol. 8, p. 50.
Chapter 1 "I Would Help You if I Could"
  1 *Testimonies*, vol. 8, p. 190.
  2 Milton Hook, *Flames Over Battle Creek* (Washington, D.C.: Review and Herald Pub. Assn., 1977), p. 98.
  3 *Medical Missionary*, October, 1895.
  4 Ellen G. White, *Special Testimonies*, Series A, No. 11, p. 21.
  5 *Medical Missionary Conference Bulletin*, May, 1899.
  6 *Medical Missionary*, February, 1906. (Italics supplied.)
  7 *General Conference Bulletin*, April 18, 1901, pp. 316, 317.
  8 Ellen G. White letter 3, 1900.
  9 *Special Testimonies*, Series B, No. 6, p. 3.
  10 *Testimonies*, vol. 8, pp. 190, 191.
Chapter 2 "We Received the Sad News"
  1 *Special Testimonies*, Series B, No. 6, p. 5.
  2 *Ibid.*, p. 9.
  3 *Ibid.*, p. 26.
  4 *The Battle Creek Sanitarium Food Idea*, Vol. I, No. 1, Nov. 15, 1902.
  5 *GC Bulletin*, 2d Quarter, 1901, p. 497.
  6 J. H. Kellogg, *The Living Temple* (Battle Creek, Mich.: Good Health Pub. Co., 1903), p. 52.
  7 See Ellen G. White Estate Document File 15 C, W. A. Spicer, "How the Spirit of Prophecy Met a Crisis," p. 21.
  8 Ellen G. White manuscript 44, 1905.
  9 Ellen G. White letter 233, 1904.
  10 D. M. Canright, *Seventh-day Adventism Renounced* (New York: Fleming H. Revell Co., 1889), p. 117.
  11 *Ibid.*, p. 413.
  12 Document File 351, letter dated July 5, 1970.
  13 Document File 15 C, Spicer, "How the Spirit of Prophecy Met a Crisis," p. 29.
  14 *Testimonies*, vol. 8, p. 97.
Chapter 3 "A Sword as of Fire"
  1 Quoted in a letter from B. P. Fairchild to A. L. White, Dec. 4, 1965.
  2 *Testimonies*, vol. 8, p. 96.
  3 *Special Testimonies*, Series B, No. 6, p. 56.
  4 A. G. Daniells, *The Abiding Gift of Prophecy* (Mountain View, Calif.: Pacific Press Pub. Assn., 1936), p. 336.
  5 Ellen G. White, *Education* (Mountain View, Calif.: Pacific Press Pub. Assn., 1903), p. 271.
  6 Daniells, *loc. cit.*
  7 *Ibid.*
  8 Letter, Ellen G. White to S. N. Haskell, Nov. 28, 1903.
  9 Daniells, *op. cit.*, p. 341.
  10 *Special Testimonies*, Series B, No. 2, pp. 21, 22.
  11 L. H. Christian, *The Fruitage of Spiritual Gifts* (Washington, D.C.: Review and Herald Pub. Assn., 1947), pp. 291, 292.
  12 Daniells, *op. cit.*, pp. 336, 337.
  13 Ellen G. White, *The Great Controversy* (Mountain View, Calif.: Pacific Press Pub. Assn., 1888), p. 425.
  14 *Ibid.* (Italics supplied.)
  15 *Testimonies*, vol. 2, p. 355.
  16 Ellen G. White, *Testimony Treasures* (Mountain View, Calif.: Pacific Press Pub. Assn., 1949), vol. 1, p. 245.
  17 Ellen G. White, *Patriarchs and Prophets* (Mountain View, Calif.: Pacific Press Pub. Assn., 1958), pp. 88, 89. (Italics supplied.)
  18 *Ibid.*, p. 89.
  19 *Testimonies*, vol. 9, p. 21.
  20 Ellen G. White, *Christ's Object Lessons* (Washington, D.C.: Review and Herald

Pub. Assn., 1900), p. 331.
[21] *The Great Controversy,* p. 489.
[22] *Ibid.*
[23] Ellen G. White, *Selected Messages* (Washington, D.C.: Review and Herald Pub. Assn., 1958), book 1, p. 382.
[24] *Special Testimonies,* Series B, No. 7, p. 37.
[25] *The Great Controversy,* p. 490.
[26] Ellen G. White letter 211, 1903.
[27] *Special Testimonies,* Series B, No. 2, p. 23.

Chapter 4 "You Are the Man . . ."
[1] Letter, A. G. Daniells to W. C. White, March 16, 1905.
[2] *Ibid.*
[3] *Ibid.*
[4] Ellen G. White manuscript 59, 1905.
[5] A. F. Ballenger, "The Nine Theses," pp. 1, 4.
[6] Ellen G. White manuscript 62, 1905.
[7] *Ibid.*
[8] A. F. Ballenger, *Cast Out for the Cross of Christ* (Tropico, Calif.: A. F. Ballenger, n.d.), p. 112.
[9] Ellen G. White manuscript 145, 1905.
[10] *Ibid.* (Italics supplied.)
[11] *Testimonies,* vol. 2, p. 171.
[12] Ellen G. White letter 201, 1899.
[13] Ellen G. White manuscript 145, 1905. (Italics supplied.)
[14] Ellen G. White manuscript 94, 1903.
[15] *Ibid.*
[16] Letter, Ellen G. White to Brethren Daniells and Prescott and their associates, Oct. 30, 1905, J. H. N. Tindall Collection.
[17] *Ibid.*
[18] *Testimonies,* vol. 5, p. 81.
[19] Letter, Ellen G. White to Brethren Daniells and Prescott and their associates, Oct. 30, 1905, J. H. N. Tindall Collection.
[20] *Selected Messages,* book 1, p. 200.
[21] *Special Testimonies,* Series B, No. 2, p. 53.

Chapter 5 Omega
[1] Eccl. 1:9. From *The Holy Bible: New International Version.* Copyright © 1978 by the New York International Bible Society. Used by permission of Zondervan Bible Publishers.
[2] *Selected Messages,* book 1, p. 197. (Italics supplied.)
[3] *Ibid.,* p. 200. (Italics supplied.)
[4] *Ibid.,* p. 204.
[5] *Ibid.,* p. 205.
[6] *Testimonies,* vol. 2, p. 355.
[7] *The Great Controversy,* p. 369.
[8] *Ibid.,* p. 370.
[9] *Special Testimonies,* Series A, No. 11, pp. 5, 6. (Italics supplied.)
[10] Ellen G. White manuscript 94, 1903. (Italics supplied.)
[11] *Ibid.* (Italics supplied.)
[12] *Special Testimonies,* Series B, No. 7, p. 30. (Italics supplied.)
[13] Letter, Ellen G. White to W. C. White, Aug. 5, 1903. (Italics supplied.)
[14] *Special Testimonies,* Series B, No. 7, p. 31. (Italics supplied.)
[15] Ellen G. White letter 328, 1906. (Italics supplied.)
[16] Letter, Ellen G. White to S. N. Haskell, Nov. 28, 1903.
[17] Ellen G. White manuscript 145, 1905. (Italics supplied.)
[18] *Selected Messages,* book 1, p. 197.
[19] *Special Testimonies,* Series B, No. 6, p. 41.
[20] *Ibid.,* p. 42.
[21] Ellen G. White letter 259, 1904.
[22] *Special Testimonies,* Series A, No. 11, pp. 9, 10.
[23] Letter, Ellen G. White to Brethren Daniells and Prescott and their associates, Oct. 30, 1905, J. H. N. Tindall Collection.
[24] *Special Testimonies,* Series A, No. 12, p. 9. (Italics supplied.)
[25] *Ibid.,* Series B, No. 7, p. 15.
[26] Letter, A. G. Daniells to W. C. White, March 16, 1905.
[27] *Selected Messages,* book 1, p. 205.
[28] *Ibid.,* p. 195.
[29] *Special Testimonies,* Series B, No. 7, p. 34.

Chapter 6 "The Test Will Come to Every Soul."
   1 *Selected Messages,* book 1, pp. 205, 206.
   2 Ellen G. White letter 328, 1906.
   3 *Testimonies,* vol. 5, p. 81.
   4 Ellen G. White, *Testimonies to Ministers* (Mountain View, Calif.: Pacific Press Pub. Assn., 1923), p. 112. (Italics supplied.)
   5 *Testimonies,* vol. 5, p. 80.
   6 Matt. 24:24; Acts 20:29, 30.
   7 *The Great Controversy,* p. 464. (Italics supplied.)
   8 *Selected Messages,* book 1, p. 48.
   9 Matt. 5:14, 16.
   10 *Testimonies,* vol. 4, p. 89.
   11 Ellen G. White, *Spiritual Gifts* (Battle Creek, Mich.: Review and Herald Pub. Assn., 1860), vol. 2, p. 284.
   12 Letter, Ellen G. White to Dr. W. H. Riley, Aug. 3, 1904.
   13 *Selected Messages,* book 1, p. 161.
   14 Letter, Ellen G. White to S. N. Haskell, Nov. 28, 1903.
   15 Ellen G. White manuscript 125, 1907.
   16 Letter, Ellen G. White to G. C. Tenney, June 29, 1906.
   17 Ellen G. White manuscript 125, 1907.
Chapter 7 Nine Salient Points
   1 *Selected Messages,* book 1, p. 195.
   2 *Ibid.,* p. 161.
   3 *Testimonies to Ministers,* p. 42. (Italics supplied.)
   4 Ellen G. White letter 138, 1902.
   5 Ellen G. White, *Counsels to Writers and Editors* (Nashville, Tenn.: Southern Pub. Assn., 1946), pp. 49, 50.
   6 *Ibid.,* p. 31.
   7 Ellen G. White manuscript 79, 1905.
   8 Letter, Ellen G. White, G. C. Tenney, June 29, 1906.
   9 *Special Testimonies,* Series B, No. 7, p. 37.
   10 Ellen G. White manuscript 20, 1906.
   11 *Selected Messages,* book 1, p. 48.
   12 Ellen G. White letter 50, 1906.
   13 *Special Testimonies,* Series B, No. 7, p. 31.
   14 Ellen G. White, *Selected Messages,* book 3, p. 84.
   15 *Ibid.,* book 1, p. 48.
   16 *Ibid.,* p. 205.
   17 *Testimonies to Ministers,* p. 474. (Italics supplied.)
   18 *Selected Messages,* book 1, p. 204.
   19 *Testimonies to Ministers,* p. 411.
   20 *Testimonies,* vol. 3, pp. 302, 303.
   21 *Ibid.,* vol. 5, p. 136.
Chapter 8 "Like a Desolating Cyclone"
   1 Canright, *op. cit.,* p. 411.
   2 *Ibid.,* p. 412.
   3 *Special Testimonies,* Series A, No. 11, p. 5. (Italics supplied.)
   4 *Ibid.,* Series B, No. 7, pp. 21, 22. (Italics supplied.)
   5 *Ibid.,* No. 6, p. 41.
   6 *Ibid.,* Series A, No. 12, p. 1.
   7 Letter, Ellen G. White to Brethren Daniells, Prescott, and their associates, Oct. 30, 1905, J. H. N. Tindall Collection.
   8 *Special Testimonies,* Series B, No. 6, pp. 42, 43.
   9 Document File 178, E. E. Andross, "Bible Study No. II," July 13, 1911, pp. 13, 14.
   10 *Testimonies,* vol. 8, p. 50.